TWO WHEELS GOOD

Paul Roberts

Order this book online at www.trafford.com
or email orders@trafford.com

Most Trafford titles are also available at major online book retailers.

Note for Librarians: A cataloguing record for this book is available from Library
and Archives Canada at www.collectionscanada.ca/amicus/index-e.html

Printed in Victoria, BC, Canada.

ISBN: 978-1-4251-8432-2

*Our mission is to efficiently provide the world's finest, most comprehensive
book publishing service, enabling every author to experience success.
To find out how to publish your book, your way, and have it available
worldwide, visit us online at www.trafford.com*

Trafford rev. 07/23/2009

North America & international
toll-free: 1 888 232 4444 (USA & Canada)
phone: 250 383 6864 ♦ fax: 250 383 6804 ♦ email: info@trafford.com

For

Ellie, Will, Tim, Nick and Francesca

With special thanks to Charlie

PART ONE

CHAPTER 1

DUNCAN POINTED THE THIN nozzle of the 3-in-One at the door hinge and squeezed the sides of the little tin but no oil appeared. Pushing his glasses onto the bridge of his nose he peered at the sealed end of the nozzle. Bracing himself on the door handle he got off his knees and sat at his desk. He leaned on the right arm of his chair, the left arm having broken sometime before his arrival at DeLouche Tutorial College. On his first day at the college he had made the mistake of leaning heavily on the broken arm and was propelled to the floor, grazing his elbow on the brass handles of his desk drawers.

He opened a long drawer in his leather topped desk and began to rummage through its contents. He removed the larger items – a padlock, two 'flick' knives, an Arabic/English dictionary, a cricket ball and three packets of 'feather-lite' condoms – and placed them on his desk top. Moving a tide of paper clips and rubber bands to the side he felt at the back of the drawer and eventually located a pair of nail scissors. Returning to the door he snipped off the pale white tip of the nozzle, knelt on the floor and squirted the oil into the hinge, working the door back and forth, the offending squeak fading with each movement. On the last swing, Duncan revealed four pairs of shoes. The worn, highly polished brogues of his employer; Nikes in a style he'd never seen before; black, toe-capped dress shoes; and stilettos with toes as lethal looking as the spiked heels. As he got up his eyes followed elegant, depilated legs until they disappeared into a black, pencil skirt.

"This is our Director of Studies – Mr Andrew. Mr Andrew – Colonel Smirka, Ivan and …"

"Secretary."

"Ah yes. Well, I'll leave you with Mr Andrew to explain the daily grind here at DeLouche."

This was a familiar moment for Duncan Andrew. Peter Rope, Principal and owner of the tutorial college, always handed over parents and their offspring to him with this line. It was intended to create an atmosphere of friendly banter but with an underly-ing assurance that the offspring would be hard at work in the college. On this occasion, the Rope line was entirely lost on the little group of Russians who now squeezed into Duncan's wood panelled office, leaving the Principal and the Director of Studies smiling absurdly, at each other.

"Well, let me tell you…." Duncan said as he wove his way past his visitors and then noticed that they were all staring at the little pile on his desk - the word 'feather-lite' seeming to be particularly visible. Colonel Smirka leant forward, the white starch of his cuff and his gold cufflinks emerging from his black Crombie overcoat as he did so. He picked up one of the knives and said:

"Tebe eti toje nyjnu?"

The secretary, who had not moved until Colonel Smirka spoke, translated his words, her expressionless face rattling out the words in a voice not dissimilar to the speaking clock.

"Must you have these too?"

"No, No. Goodness, no".

Duncan looked at the sullen face of Ivan and the massy bulk of his father, whose face appeared to have been the victim of an acid attack, its pasty folds pockmarked with small craters. He thought he might make a joke about all the things he had in his drawer but changed his mind, swept the items back into the drawer and closed it. Duncan turned his attention to Ivan who seemed to him to be a potent brew of testosterone and adolescent resentment.

"Well Ivan, so you would like to study with us."

The youth shrugged and folded his arms across his chest.

"Uniwercity."

When Colonel Smirka spoke the secretary began to speak again, as if his voice activated her automatically. Duncan wondered what else she did automatically for him.

"We are pleased that Ivan has a place at your illustrious university. We are prepared to negotiate more money if that is required."

"Um. Yes. Ivan will have to pass some examinations before he can go to any university in Britain."

The room was suddenly filled with an electronic version of the Ride of the Valkyries and Ivan reached into his leather jacket and held his mobile to his ear.

"Da. Ten o'clock. Bring it."

"As I was saying. I think you may have the wrong impression."

Duncan's heart sank.

"Uniwercity."

"Mr Rope has assured us that everything will be possible. Ivan must have the degree before returning to Minsk where he will take over from his father as the imde," said Colonel Smirka's secretary.

"Imde?"

"Imde," the secretary repeated.

Duncan gave up.

"And how is your English, Ivan?"

Once again, Ivan shrugged his shoulders. His heavy face was a relatively unblemished and younger version of his father's. He sat with his hands clasped to the chair as if he expected to be tipped out of it at any moment. A gold bracelet fell over the face of his Rolex watch. Ivan noticed that Duncan had seen his watch and became animated.

"You wint? I got you. Genuine fake."

Colonel Smirka growled something in Russian to his son as if he were bringing a dog to heel.

"I think we should start with an English course, don't you? What do you hope to study at university?"

Colonel Smirka looked at his watch and stared at Duncan while he and the secretary had a hurried exchange.

"Colonel Smirka expects his son to graduate in Bwisness in three year's time. He thanks you for your time and says that you must be Ivan's father in his absence."

"Oh, well. We'll do our best I am sure."

He smiled weakly as Colonel Smirka came forward and crushed Duncan's hand in his before backing out of the room. Duncan was unsure whether this was from force of habit being reluctant to put himself in an unguarded position or whether his huge frame could not turn without causing damage in Duncan's cramped office. The secretary stood up and straightened her skirt.

"Colonel Smirka is attending a reception to honour his contribution to the new bwisness school. We will leave Ivan with you. It will not be possible to contact Colonel Smirka when he returns to Chechnya. Here is the number of his London office."

With that her solemn face broke into a seraphic smile and she, too, was gone. The Wagnerian jingle burst from Ivan's pocket again and a brief exchange followed.

"I must leave. Bwisness."

Duncan had time to see Ivan's mobile screen saver before he snapped the little instrument shut – the picture was a cartoon bear on its hind legs holding a fistful of dollar bills in each paw. Ivan was clearly making a start on the career his father had in mind for him. Duncan wondered what kind of business Ivan might be engaged in. His thoughts were interrupted by the appearance of his Principal escorting a woman and her daughter along the corridor between their two offices. The walls of the dim corridor were hung with eighteenth century prints of college buildings. Figures in academic gowns stood in the foreground. The floor of the corridor was uneven, the rucked surface of an old sisal carpet adding to its hazardous character.

"Mind your head. This beam often catches us out."

Peter Rope was five foot two and had no need to duck and was never caught out by the beam or anything else. However, it was an opportunity to underline the quaint nature of the college which he had spent his working life developing. As a marketer of education he had realized at an early stage the deep attraction a certain image held for parents. While Rope himself had attended a comprehensive school in his native Cannock, he had soon understood that a combination of beamed buildings, worn carpets, leather chairs, a touch of Louise XV and oak furniture was a potent aphrodisiac for those seeking an exclusive education for their children.

Mrs Daphne Bowler was a large woman with wild graying hair and what used to be called grog blossom clearly evident on her nose and cheeks.

"Dysexlia."

"I beg your pardon?"

"Dyslexia. There's your problem. No idea where she gets it from, although her father was a bit dappy, lovely pair of legs though. Dylexic. Always has been. Not that anyone took any notice. Bain of yer life, hasn't it bin? Louisa. Louisa."

The tall teenager at Mrs Bowler's side had been gazing around the room while her mother spoke, her index finger exploring the inside of her left nostril in a contemplative way. When her mother called her name for the second time she seemed to shake all over like a wet dog. She raked a bony hand across her unkempt hair.

"Ya."

And her eyes wondered off again, her fingers once again probing her nose and then her mouth and then her ears.

"She got a couple of the levels but really no thanks to the LEA and no thanks to the bloody schools either."

"Schools?"

"Six of them to date. All promising this and that. Useless. Took the LEA to appeal. Lost, despite a water tight ed. psych. report. One of the few exams she's passed with flying colours, eh, Louisa?

Shouldn't laugh really. Anyway, we've got funding now and here we are."

Louisa shivered again and pointed to a brightly tasselled woven medallion hanging on Duncan's wall, its reds and blues at odds with the discoloured yellow of his walls.

"What's that?"

"It's a Korean charm."

"Cool."

Mrs Bowler fired a barrage of questions at Duncan and jabbed her finger at paragraphs in Louisa's educational psychologist's report underlined in red. Louisa's learning difficulties were itemized with a perverse pride and Duncan was told that Louisa's teachers would have to ensure that she was given extra time to complete notes and that any distractions would mean that Louisa would be unable to concentrate. Her teachers would also have to expect her to turn up to tutorials at the wrong time, even on the wrong day (here Mrs Bowler stopped and turned to her daughter letting out a loud guffaw of laughter) and that allowances would have to be made for late and incomplete work. She fell silent for a moment and then said:

"Well, I think that's more or less it."

Louisa dug her mother in her arm and Mrs Bowler looked at her watch.

"Oh, God. He'll have given up on me by now."

"I'm sorry?" said Duncan.

"Mum's boyfriend," said Louisa.

"Toy boy more like, Ha! Gorgeous eyes, " said Mrs Bowler.

"She's always late for things. You'd better go, Mum."

Alone again, Duncan closed his office door and stood by the window. Some students and one or two tutors were enjoying a break in the small, sun filled courtyard opposite the college building. From where he was standing Duncan could also see over the wall that divided the college from the street beyond.

Duncan raised his hand and waved at a figure slumped in the doorway of the night shelter over the street.

"Morning, George."

George, who had been staring up at the window, put a small bottle into the pocket of his frayed overcoat and waved back. Duncan was on friendly terms with several of the drunks and homeless who turned up at the hostel for food or shelter or both. He felt a kind of empathy with these lost souls and would say to himself after passing the time of day with George or any of the others, 'there but for the grace of God go I'. For Duncan this was more than a platitude – he genuinely felt that there was very little between him and destitution, that the trappings of security could very easily be whipped away from him and that he would find himself sitting next to George on the pavement and waving up at the new Director. As he stood at the window, he was overwhelmed by a feeling that had dogged him his whole adult life. He was a fake, a chancer, someone pretending to be a responsible adult, someone who would eventually be found out, frogmarched to the door and hurled into outer darkness. This feeling was particularly virulent now as he looked down at George, possibly because of the interviews that morning.

Duncan opened the slim lid of his lap top. Glancing down his e-mail list he saw jumbo41@hotmail.com. Jumbo was the tag name his son had invented when he set off on his gap year trip some three months before.

Dear parental units I'm now in Phang Bok long boat ride to here but it's great. Sonny and I had to play snooker with the head man before he would allow us to stay. I made sure we didn't beat him – thought this might have been the wrong thing to do! The beach was terrible, full of people like us and all thinking they were really cool Sonny's shoes fell to bits but someone in the village fixed him up from bits of an old tyre. It's raining. Moving on tomorrow to Dal Lat to see the dragons what id give for one night in my old bed but having an excellent time met an Aussie yesterday who eats fire. Really. Love Simon.

Duncan forwarded the e-mail to his wife and then moved the arrow to 'Reply'

Dear Simon good to hear from you. Don't forget – avoid Lom Bok at all costs. FO guidance is pretty clear. Nasty place. Your mother and I are fine. Sarah playing up – she didn't come in till gone 2.00 the other night and didn't seem at all apologetic. Ah, the joys of parenting. Nothing much to report, usual round of dinners and domestic tasks. By the way, did you take my moleskin note book? I can't find it anywhere. Look after yourself. Love Dad.

Duncan clicked on send and opened his saved documents. Scrolling through the list he found an unfinished document – 'Staff Handbook'. He sighed and began to tap in sentences.

CHAPTER 2

THE TRAP GROUND ALLOTMENTS sparkled with early morning dew. Here and there shed roofs shone in the bright sunlight. The burst husks of last year's runner beans hung limp and sodden from improvised frameworks. The business of clearing the winter debris was almost complete and the curved backs of allotment holders bent to their self appointed tasks. The throaty sound of a rotavator disturbed the air, its blades turning over the compacted soil in readiness for planting. Lindsey North closed the galvanized metal gate that the allotment association had recently installed.

"Morning."

A man with wild grey hair and a brussel sprout stalk in each gloved hand greeted Lindsey as he made his way along the grassy path.

"I see the codswallopers have visited us again."

He waved one of the gnarled stalks in the direction of a large hole. There were several similar holes dotted about the Trap Grounds bearing witness to the nocturnal visits of gangs of men in search of Victorian glass bottles.

"I'm amazed they think it's worth it."

"Yes, bad business," Lindsey said with barely concealed indifference.

"Time to be getting runners in."

The man looked at Lindsey's suede loafers and immaculate Diesel jeans and suspected that he was not in the presence of a serious fellow planter.

"Yes. Runners."

Lindsey reached an area of ground where the allotments were particularly neglected, the last members having thrown in the towel realizing that keeping on top of their land required a medieval devotion that even the strong motivators of guilt and envy that kept the others at their hoes had, in the end, not been enough. These lapsed members had fled in the face of a rising tide of weed and chiropractors' bills leaving Lindsey's corner undisturbed by reminders that it was either too early or too late to plant runners or any other vegetable. He approached a shed that had the same dilapidated appearance as all the others in the Trap Grounds. The shed was secured by a padlock and a heavy duty bolt. Moving a little brass plate he inserted a key in the eye of the lock. . Moving the bolt along its metal track he jerked the shed door open. An inner door was now revealed, this time not made of tongue and groove boxwood, but two inch thick sheet metal. He opened this door and a light came on automatically. He pulled the wooden door behind him and then the inner door, locking them both. Moving with habitual ease, Lindsey fitted a pair of headphones to his ears and sat before a rolltop console. Pushing the rolltop into its casing, he was presented with rows of dials and display lights. He opened a little notebook and tapped in some numbers to a key pad. Tiny LED lights came on and he sat back. After a brief pause an assortment of letters appeared on a screen and, working between the screen and his note- book, Lindsey began to make notes.

CHAPTER 3

"Bugger, Bugger, Bugger."

Duncan stood in the little courtyard and dug his hands into his anorak. He turned his keys in his pocket and walked up and down along the line of bikes that were leaning against the wall. His bike was definitely not there. For a moment he wondered if he had walked to work that morning. He dismissed this possibility when he remembered that Claire, his wife, had stopped him at the garden gate before he left home. She had kissed him on the cheek and then put three letters into the hinged rack behind his seat. Stopping at the end of his road, he had reached across the pavement to post the letters. There was no doubt that he had ridden his bike through the city centre to work and there was no doubt that his bike was no longer where he had left it that morning. Duncan pushed open the gate to the courtyard and held it open with his foot.

"Another day, another dollar, Mr Duncan."

"George, have you been here all day?"

"Mostly, Mr D. I did slip off for a bit to test the charitable instincts of the people of this fair city but otherwise I have been like patience on a monument."

"It's just that …"

A van turned down the narrow street between the college and the night shelter and for a moment Duncan lost sight of George.

"It's just that someone has taken my bike and I wondered if you had seen anything, anyone wheeling it away."

"No. No."

George got to his feet, his shambling figure spilling folds of worn, grey material as he straightened and came across to where Duncan stood.

"Lots of people come and go. Now let me see. There was a young feller moved away quick about 10.00 but not on your bike, then there was the delivery about 11.30. Of course…"

Duncan was enveloped in the musty, sweet breath of the alcoholic. He listened with diminishing interest as George catalogued the arrivals and departures of the day. The homeless man had taken on the role of unofficial gatekeeper and despite the effects of alcohol, had an extraordinary ability to recall any movements to and from the college.

"Must have been while I was fillin' the cap. I've let you down Mr D and I'm truly sorry."

"Well never mind. Too late now. Enough cash for the night?"

"Yes, yes. They'll be lettin' us in soon. I've got plenty."

"Goodnight then."

"Goodnight, sweet prince."

Duncan moved away up the street and joined the hurrying crowds of office workers and shop assistants that swirled and eddied along the main street. He wove past the blank faces of people waiting at a line of bus stops and breathed in the hot air blown into his face from shop doors. Stopping at a kiosk he queued behind a man who wore a dayglo tabard with the letters BT stamped on the back. Duncan watched the girl in the kiosk. She smiled at her next customer, her pale skin made translucent by the fluorescent light above her head. She reached into a little glass cabinet and took out the last of the day's flapjacks. He noticed how the girl blew away strands of her hair by expelling air out of the side of her mouth. She turned a black wheel on the front of the stainless steel coffee machine and steam hissed into a cardboard cup.

"Chocolate or nutmeg?"

The girl's voice, soft and Irish and slow. That's what he'd been waiting for and maybe a smile as well. Duncan shifted his pannier into his free hand and moved to the front of the queue. He looked up at the girl. There was something about looking up at her, as if she were dispensing more than just cappuccino. The slow movement of the line, the patient silence of those waiting to be fed and comforted, the pattern of her movement from cabinet, to machine, to counter, to cash till and the final conferring of change and a 'thank you, goodnight'. He thought about rituals and religious observance and felt at peace. Duncan was tired, wanted to get home, was not thirsty or hungry and yet he waited in the queue and then placed his order.

"A cappuccino, please."

"Large, medium or small?"

"Small, please."

He wondered why he was here looking up at the Irish girl as she prepared his order. It was nothing to do with peace and religion and probably everything to do with just wanting to ogle the girl. He often stopped here and sometimes he had tried to engage her in conversation but she had never responded. She must, he thought, recognize him by now, but she never showed this.

"Chocolate or nutmeg?"

"Chocolate, please. Oh and don't worry about the top, I'll…"

"Thank you, good night."

Now it was someone else's turn. Duncan held the cardboard cup by the rim and picked up his pannier. He was irritated by having to carry two things now, irritated by his own voice, by the redundancy of his language: 'Please, thank you, please, thank you.'

He sat on a low wall and put his pannier between his legs. He blew gently on the froth so that it trembled and then he sucked it in noisily, the hot coffee hitting the roof of his mouth and making him wince. A party of French school children moved past him, their chatter making a wall of sound. When they had gone Duncan found himself staring at Mrs Bowler who was emerging from a wine bar across the street. A young man was behind her holding the door open with his outstretched arm. As she passed him she threw her head back and laughed at something he said. Duncan was particularly good at seeing people he knew before they saw him. He often used this ability to evade encounters and took a curious pleasure in observing his quarry before turning away. Indeed, he often challenged himself to look at the person for as long as possible, timing his escape to the last second before they turned to acknowledge him. Later, when he saw the person again, they would say 'I saw you the other day in …' and he would reply vaguely 'Oh, did you. Did I ignore you?' and they would laugh. Once, he mistimed his move and was caught staring at Mr Gill, the printer who did all the college prospectuses. They had chatted for a while but Duncan could see that Mr Gill was wondering why the Director had been looking at him so intently. Occasionally, Duncan wondered about this habit as well but this little game amused him and took his mind off his humdrum existence. He took in Mrs Bowler and her young companion and wondered how long he had got. They were too close for him to move away unnoticed but perhaps, if he looked away at the right moment… Mrs Bowler waited for her companion to struggle into his leather jacket. His neck and head seemed all of one, tapered piece. His chiselled face and shaved head were small and out of proportion to the rest of his body, the thick muscle-bound neck straining the white collar of his starched shirt. Mrs Bowler took hold of his arm and, before Duncan could look away, marched across the street to where he sat. Duncan struggled to his feet, flecks of coffee spilling from his cup.

"Mr Duncan?"

"Andrew."

"Ah. Off duty. I understand. Andrew, this is Josh. Josh, Andrew."

"No, um."

"Mate."

"How do you do?"

"Are you alright? You look a bit shocked," said Mrs Bowler.

"No I'm fine. Fine."

"Lovely to have an afternoon off and to manage to drag Josh here away from the gym. I've got a good lot at the moment."

"A good lot?"

Duncan was having difficulty keeping up with Mrs Bowler's mental twists and turns.

"Yes, managers. I'm Two Wheels Good – you know, biking holidays for the adventurous spirit. Do you like biking, Andrew?"

"Well, I did, but …."

"Very popular in these parts. We've been having a drink. Saw you from the window. Thanks for taking the daughter in, she's a sweet girl but drives me round the bend. Ha! On your way home?"

Josh shifted from foot to foot and gazed over Duncan's shoulder while Mrs Bowler spoke, his eyes scanning the late shoppers who spilled onto the street from a department store behind him.

"Yes on foot I'm afraid. Someone stole my bike today."

He had no need to tell anyone this but he could think of nothing else to say. Mrs Bowler fired questions at him and he felt like a schoolboy who had been careless.

"Well, I'm just as bad. Losing things all the time. Car keys, shopping lists, addresses, husbands. Ha! Still there are compensations for the latter."

Mrs Bowler looked at Josh and ran a hand over his shaved dome. With her free hand she wound the end of a pashmina scarf around her wrist.

"Yeah. Lot of it about," said Josh.

Whether Josh was referring to the theft of his bike or his relationship to Mrs Bowler was not clear, but with this they turned away. Duncan watched them move up the street and then turn into a hotel entrance. Duncan imagined their afternoon of passion in one of the small bedrooms in the Hotel Morton. The thought of Mrs Bowler's fleshy bulk lying on a candlewick counterpane while the toned body of Josh stalked the room finishing his cigarette before he set to work made Duncan feel uncomfortable. He imagined Josh winding her pashmina around her wrists and tying them to an iron bedhead while Mrs Bowler barked instructions at her lover.

Duncan remembered that he had to drop in at one of the halls of residence for the college before he went home. Cynthia Digit was the senior housemother with whom he had to make arrangements for the college outing scheduled for the following weekend. She provided the 'tea' after the outing, usually a punting trip for any students that wanted to come. Duncan reached the tree- lined road that led out of the city centre and began to walk towards the Victorian villa where twenty one of DeLouche's students lived. He walked past the garish baskets hanging from cast iron lamp-posts every fifteen feet along the road, labels announcing their sponsorship by Savoury's Estate Agency clearly visible amongst the pom-pom blooms.

*

Cynthia Digit was standing at the door when Duncan arrived. The doorway and the whole building had an ecclesiastical feel; the porch and all the windows had elongated arches, framed by slim pillars set into the brick work.

"Hello, dear. Not on your bike?"

Duncan resisted the temptation to go through the story again and said:

"I've come about the outing."

Cynthia Digit led Duncan into her boudoir. Dim lighting and silk drapes combined with the sickly aroma of joss sticks gave the room a distinctly 'hippie' feel. Moving a worn copy of 'Zen and the Art of Motorcycle Maintenance' and the remains of a chicken supper, the housemother beckoned the director to sit on her sofa. The sofa was covered in a hand woven blanket of deep blue and had little glass stars and moons stitched onto its surface. Two Siamese cats watched Duncan from a window seat crowded with multicoloured cushions.

"Where are we going this year, dear?"

"I thought a punting party."

"Now, there's a good idea."

They both laughed. In fact, the DeLouche College outings were always punting parties. It was held after the start of term as a way of bringing the new students together and gave Duncan an opportunity to show off his skills as a puntsman.

Cynthia Digit lit a menthol cigarette and launched herself at an easy chair, curling her left leg underneath her as she sat. She was in her late fifties and had been a statuesque beauty in her time but now her unkempt hair fell in ochre swatches down her back which was showing the first signs of curvature of the spine. She had been part of the generation that had made its way to India in the nineteen sixties and had lived in an ashram before following her boyfriend, Doug Digit to a small apartment in Height Ashbury. Surrounded by anti-war posters and the paraphernalia of political protest she had lived in squalid happiness until the day Doug had been hit by a Greyhound bus leaving Cynthia a widow of very little means.

There was a knock at the door and a tearful girl appeared saying that she simply had to speak to Cynthia. The girl threw herself into a chair, covered her face with her hands and sobbed loudly. Cynthia sat on the arm of the chair and appeared to know what was coming next. The girl stopped sobbing and looked up at Cynthia. There was a moment's silence and then a torrent of anguished words poured from her lips.　　During this interlude Duncan felt invisible, as if the very nature of their conversation, the twists and turns of Miranda's love life, were a female preoccupation from which he, a mere male, was excluded. He turned his attention to a framed photo in the centre of the mantelpiece. It showed a battered yellow VW 'Combi' van on a desert road with a young man – Duncan assumed that this was Cynthia's husband – leaning against the bonnet of the van. He was wearing a long, embroidered kaftan and had the drooping moustaches of his time. Strands of his long hair blew across his face so that with the moustache, it was difficult to see his expression. Here, Duncan thought, was youth and hope and freedom. At the bottom of the photo someone had written: 'Mohave Desert, 1968'.

Having received sage advice from her housemother, Miranda wiped her eyes and prepared to leave.

"Thanks Mrs D – you're the best."

Miranda hugged Cynthia Digit, glanced briefly at her Director of Studies as if she had only just noticed him and left the room.

"What?" Cynthia said.

"What would we do without you, Mrs D?"

Cynthia smiled and they got down to the serious business of planning the college outing.

CHAPTER 4

DUNCAN CLOSED THE GARDEN gate behind him. He had recently had a high fence installed, the Mendip gate allowing the passer-by a glimpse of the garden but no more. He stood for a moment enjoying his invisibility from the road. Putting his briefcase down he cleared lengths of eucalyptus bark from the garden path. Claire and he had planted the tree after their return from a summer holiday in Cornwall. Their rented cottage had been surrounded by eucalyptus' and so they had gone to the garden centre that autumn, bought the tree and planted it. Daffodils lined the garden path to the front door. Most of the flower heads were blotched with brown and Duncan set to work separating the stems and looping them into loose knots. He pinched any stems that still supported a fresh flower and gathered them together in a bunch to put in a vase and place on Claire's dressing table. He inspected a mixed line of berberis and forsythia shrubbery. The idea had been to screen the drive but he had not planted enough, so that now the racemes of golden and yellow flowers appeared threadbare and inadequate. He had told Claire that it was a 'work in progress' and made a note to 'feed' the shrubbery at the weekend.

Duncan opened the front door and picked up the letters from the morning delivery. Claire left for work before him and he was the first home at the end of the day. Sorting the letters was always the first thing he did when he returned from work. One of the letters had the clear imprint of a Doc Marten boot running diagonally across its surface. Sarah, sixteen and not as sweet as he had hoped she would be at that age, was the only other person who might have picked the letters up but this would have shown a degree of awareness that Duncan realized she had not yet attained. The footprint was evidence, at least, that she had left the house at some point in the day although it could not be assumed that she had arrived at school. Duncan filled a kettle and placed it on the hob. He spread the letters on the kitchen island and opened an adjacent cupboard door. As he did this the paper recycling bin was pulled forward on its tracks. There were three potential categories of mail: his, Claire's and junk mail. On this occasion the recycling bin received a flier which read "Too Busy to Clean?" offering domestic services; a Bupa pamphlet bearing the unctuous heading "Because you deserve to get better"; and a folded card in the shape of a tetrapack advertising Tropicana's latest deals. Duncan's pile consisted of a bill from BT and a reminder from the Water Board that he had not paid for that half. Claire's mail included an A4 pack from The Hedge Fund Manager, a professional journal to which she subscribed; a flier advertising a production of 'A Doll's House' at The Playhouse, and two handwritten envelopes that Duncan recognized as belonging to clients. Duncan put a teabag into a mug and poured water from the kettle until the teabag rose to the rim of the mug. He put Claire's letters in her study and made his way to the top of the house. The loft conversion that had followed the reinstatement of the Andrew household as 'dual income' when Claire returned to full-time work after the birth of their children was where Duncan had established his den. He pushed open the Velux window and breathed in the late spring air. The distant hum of the ring road was not loud enough to spoil this moment of peace. The window allowed him an uninterrupted view along Kingston Road and into the back gardens of the terraced housing that stretched its length. Duncan watched builders emerging from the front door of one of the houses pushing rubble filled barrows and running them up planks attached to the back of a skip. The process of gentrifying these Victorian railway workers' cottages was not confined to one house. Duncan counted four 'Mick's Skips' along the road and remembered a time when Claire and he were students. They had been staying with a friend of Claire's who was at the university and who had digs on Kingston Road. They had slept on a pile of old mattresses and had woken in the morning to the sight of silver fish swarming over the floor. This bohemian world was now disappearing to be replaced by the comforts of en suite bathrooms and the chic of Poggenpohl. He emptied the contents of his briefcase onto his desk and pressed the answer button on his phone.

"Oh, hello, is Bridget here. I can't come do the cleaning today. I sick."

Delete.

"Hello, Mr and Mrs Andrew. It's Catherine Pike here from School. I'm Sarah's Head of Year. We were wondering if there was any reason why Sarah had not been in school today or yesterday. Could you give me a ring – I'm on 933742. Thanks."

Next.

"Are you paying too much for your …"

Duncan cut the message off and thought that whatever it was he was undoubtedly paying too much but felt sure that there was no help at hand. He arranged his work for the evening on the desk – six UCAS references to be completed that evening due to the pathological inability of some of his students to meet deadlines and three letters to be written to parents. Finally, he smoothed a crumpled piece of paper onto the laminated surface of his desk and tried to make out the figures and spidery letters that Sylvie, the college secretary, had written. They had had a conversation earlier that day in which she had complained to him about pay and leave. Sylvie had handed this scrap of paper to him as he left the office asking him to look it over. Sylvie's touching belief in his ability to put things right was doubly misguided. In the first place he could understand none of the things that she had so carefully noted down and in the second place his failure to stand up to his employer was one of the guilty secrets he kept to himself when he was drawn into office gossip by anyone with an axe to grind against Principal Rope. The fact was that Duncan was just as capable of agreeing with his employer when he railed against the inefficiency and mendacity of those he employed. Duncan tried to rationalize this fence sitting insincerity by telling himself that none of it mattered to him, that he was above office politics. In reality, his need to please everyone was a treatable condition that he had glimpsed during a brief flirtation with psychoanalysis and which he was happier now to overlook.

*

"What shall we have?" asked Claire.

Duncan opened the double doors of the fridge and considered what he and Claire might concoct for dinner.

"I put the brisket in about an hour ago."

"There are some of those mushrooms from the French market at the back of the fridge somewhere. Oh, and the courgettes. I got some with the florets so you could do your special."

Duncan pulled out the brown paper bag containing the mushrooms. The bag was soggy.

"Will these be OK?"

Claire took off her coat and came to stand next to Duncan. She kissed him and put her arm around him. Their faces were lit up by the fridge lights.

"They're fine. How were things in the groves of academe today?"

"Plus ca change. Mrs Pike phoned."

"Who?"

"Sarah's Head of Year."

"Oh, yes. Sarah phoned me this morning and said she wasn't going to school today – she was going to work at Bridie's house."

"Ah yes, the partner in crime."

"Bridie's a nice girl – she's the only one keeping Sarah on track."

Duncan opened a bag of new potatoes and poured them into a stainless steel pan. He filled the pan with cold water and placed it beside the cooker.

"Simon e-mailed. He seems to be surviving. I must tell him about the bucket."

"Bucket?"

Claire placed a round chopping board on the island and began to cut the thick stem from the base of broccoli heads.

"Yes, I was speaking to a student today who'd just come back from Indonesia. Apparently there's some concoction that's passed around in a big bucket and they all drink from it – this chap said he knew someone who'd contracted hepatitis from it. Pass me the frying pan."

Duncan moved the broccoli stems to one side and, selecting another knife, began to separate the coruscated yellow florets from a heap of courgettes that Claire had put at his side.

"And you, the day?"

"I had to stand all the way to Paddington again and the train stopped outside Reading for twenty unexplained minutes so I missed my call from New York. This sub prime business is doing very funny things to the market. We haven't felt the half of it yet."

Duncan opened a glass fronted cupboard and took a wine glass from the shelf. He poured wine from an open bottle and slid it across the kitchen island to Claire. Sipping the wine she passed him a bag of flour. He shook the white powder into a mixing bowl, the residue rising into the air and dusting his hands and arms. He dripped water into the bowl and began to mix it until it was neither too liquid nor too firm.

"Cynthia and I have sorted the picnic out for next weekend. D'you want to come?"

"I can't. There's a symposium, work needs me to go. D'you mind?"

"No, no."

Duncan plunged one of the florets into the flour and water and held it there for longer than was strictly necessary. Claire poured a stream of amber liquid into the frying pan until there was an inch of extra virgin warming in the pan.

"It's too late to call Mrs Pike. Can you do it tomorrow?"

"Yup. How's the oil coming?"

Claire peered into the pan and watched as the oil began to move, its viscous surface forming and reforming in marbled waves.

"Almost ready."

Claire told Duncan about her lunch with the directors and then described the day's dealings in the language of the city. Duncan rummaged through a basket of vegetables and only half listened as Claire spoke about fixed income security transactions, trading volumes and emerging market bonds. He chose his favourite little knife and began to peel away the encrusted surface of carrots. He heard her mention derivatives and knew that they had some bearing on doms or was it non-doms?

"The legal position of non-doms is changing now. It'll be interesting to see how that affects their portfolio profiles."

Duncan ran his knife along the now bright orange surface of one of the carrots and thought about non-doms and condoms. Claire went on and he listened and nodded and asked the odd question and thought that her words had a certain poetry to them – short selling, futures, venture capital and leverage all had a physicality that reflected the daily world in which she moved. He thought about the city and its centuries of trade. He imagined the Golden Hind tied up in the Pool of London laden with fardels of cloth and pokes of wool and chests of pewterware, while other craft were piloted into safe moorings and the business of unloading stockfish or iron ore mined in the Cantabrian mountains got under way within earshot of the beating hammers and the industrial fires of St Katherine's and Wapping. Duncan cleared pans and utensils away and stared out of the kitchen window and weighed anchor with Martin Frobisher and Francis Drake and curled his arms around the rat lines that led away from the mizzen of the good ship Ivy bound for the cod fields of Iceland. He watched as the ship swung away from the victuallers and shipwrights that crowded the river bank and the pilot steered them past the pirates who hung in chains awaiting their fate at high tide. He watched as the side of the little wooden ship was reflected in the glass flanks of the Legal and General building at Limehouse and the shining tower at Canary Wharf and looked astern for a last glimpse of the steeple of St Paul's before turning and turning again to make Blackwall Reach and then the mudflats of Essex and the salt marshes of Kent.

"Duncan? Have you gone to sleep?"

"Sorry. Off with the fairies. What's next?"

He wondered, not for the first time, whether he was not quite up to the mark, had not 'got on' sufficiently in life and had a mental picture of himself sitting next to George on the pavement outside DeLouche College, it having been discovered that his capacity to manage anything was limited to the point of invisibility.

Duncan wondered why Claire had not gone off with some rakish trader- a man with a future in futures. They stood side by side and dropped the soaking florets into the pan and watched them as they curled and wrinkled.

CHAPTER 5

"Who's got a bottle opener?"

Giles Fairfax held up the required openers, one in each hand. Duncan approved of Giles who was a hard working student with just a whiff of glamour about him having joined DeLouche after a hurried departure from Eton College the exact circumstances of which were not known.

"I thought we'd better have two – one for each boat."

"Good man, Giles. I think that qualifies you as the commander of the second punt."

The punt party stood on the sloping 'hard' surrounded by the paraphernalia of the outing. Travelling blankets were slung over shoulders and plastic bags, heavy with food, were passed from hand to hand. At their feet wicker baskets, cool boxes, golfing brollies and a guitar case. Duncan directed some of the students to fetch paddles and cushions and to carry the unwieldy punt poles down to the water. He saw Ivan standing slightly apart from the rest and called to him to fetch some cushions but he did not respond. After he had asked him again Duncan realized that earphones and 'gangsta rap' were preventing him from carrying out any requests. Someone tapped Duncan on the shoulder.

"Ah, Class. Civ, there you are. Glad you could make it."

"Watcha. Wouldn't miss it for worlds. It's me fav'rit Odyssey is this."

The dishevelled figure of Steve Durrant, tutor and scholar of the ancient world, stood above Duncan and beamed at him.

"Good turn out. Oo else is comin'?"

"I'm expecting Pandora and er, Lindsey. Sylvie's over there. It's her day off but she's claiming it on her holiday roster. Do watch out, Louisa."

A long length of punt pole emerged from the dark interior of the boat house, its end tapping on the concrete as Louisa struggled to hold it above the ground. Moving along the pole she jerked it into the air, snagging the wide brim of Cynthia Digit's summer hat. Too late to catch it she watched if fill with air and float away from her. Giles grabbed one of the paddles and set off in pursuit, bringing the hat to ground just before it was lost over the water.

"Bravo, Giles."

Two bikes appeared at the gate to the boathouse, their riders dismounting and fitting bike locks. Pandora Fulbright waved a delicate hand at Duncan and made her way towards him. The other rider tilted his handle mirror, rearranged his hair and, slinging a canvas bag over his shoulder, followed Pandora. Duncan noticed that two of his female students turned as he approached, hoping, he assumed, that the new arrival would notice them.

"Thanks for coming, Pandora, Lindsey. We're all here now. We can go."

An excited mayhem followed as decisions were made and coun-
termanded as to who would go with whom. Lindsey's admir-
ers took him by the arms and marched him to one of the punts
amidst giggles and feigned protests. Cynthia organized the other
students into a chain and they passed the picnic along the line
and into the punts.

"Wrong boat. They've already got beer"

"Who wants this summer pudding?"

"Careful, that one's got cake in it."

"We forgot plates."

Bags and belongings were passed back and forth over the gunwales
amidst mock recriminations and shrieks. When everyone was
settled Giles and Duncan wheeled their punt poles and moved
into the middle of the river. As they turned they saw a punt arriving and an elderly woman was being lifted onto the duck boards.
She was soaked and ashen and missing one shoe, grey river slime
streaked across her face and shoulders. Her shoulders heaved with
short breaths, one hand held over her heart. A waiter appeared
from the punt station restaurant and moved down the slope with
a glass of whisky in his hand. Duncan dug his pole into the
water and his punt moved forward, the last thing he saw was the
woman reaching up to take the glass, the flesh and muscles on her
arm slack and mottled. Duncan and Giles nodded at each other
and began to establish a rhythm.

Pandora, her hand clamped firmly on the side of the punt, was
wedged between the side of the punt and the solid mass that was
Steve Durrant.

"Can't you make it stop wobbling, Duncan?"

Pandora smiled nervously and tightened her grip even more.

"Have no fear Miss Fulbright, you're in the hands of a master puntsman."

"And where is our illustrious boss?" said Steve.

"Mr Rope? Declared himself unavailable."

"Surprise, surprise."

"Now then, don't bite the hand that feeds you," said Duncan.

"'Ardly," said Steve.

Moorhens fussed on their nests and fresh willow mopped the water. Hands trailed in the current.

"Duck everyone, there's a branch just ahead."

The passengers slid down on their cushions, Lindsey's companions nestled even closer to him. Lindsey's arms snaked around their backs, holding them to him.

"Oh, Lindsey this is cosy. You can't escape us now."

"Nor do I want to my lovelies."

Duncan watched as the girls shrieked with laughter and squirmed under Lindsey's predatory arms. He looked away. Cynthia waved from her boat, her other hand stroking Louisa's hair as she lay asleep at her side. Duncan thought that the childless Cynthia had found the perfect outlet for her motherly instincts in becoming a housemother at DeLouche.

"Perfect weather, Duncan. How clever of you to arrange it."

"I think my line to the almighty was cut some time ago, Mrs Digit."

"I've never seen you as a great sinner, Duncan."

"No, I think He just lost interest in me."

Sylvie eased the cork from a bottle of Cava and shot it across the water where it 'pinged' against one of the cool boxes in Duncan's boat. She filled a slender glass and raised it above her head.

"A direct hit."

"An unprovoked attack. Revenge!"

One of Lindsey's lovelies unleashed another cork which struck Sylvie on the cheek.

"Ow, that hurt."

"Sorry Sylvie, sorry, sorry."

Giles steered his punt further away. Pandora fidgeted, crossing and uncrossing her legs and stared at the bank. Steve clambered over the ménage a trois grabbing a paddle as he went. He kneeled on the front of the punt and paddled.

"How's mother, Pandora? Well, I hope."

"Thanks for asking, Duncan. She's not really that good. I need help with her. Social services send someone every so often but they're more of a hindrance than a help. It's her nerves, she can't settle and doesn't seem to know where she is half the time. The other day she asked me who I was."

"Worrying."

"Yes. There's no one else, you see. Just me. She's beginning to, you know, lose control as well. It's wearing."

"Sorry to hear that. This must be a nice break."

Pandora craned her neck and Duncan looked at her pale, upside down face. A vein at the side of her eye pulsed.

"Oh, it's wonderful. Just being here. With you. All."

"Good."

Duncan drove his pole deep into the soft river bed to propel the punt forward but it stuck and the punt was brought to a shuddering halt as Duncan struggled to extract it. The lovelies screamed and Steve grabbed the back of Lindsey's shirt to steady himself. Two buttons were ripped out of their holes revealing the blond hair on Lindsey's chest.

"Oo, how manly. Can we feel?"

"This is a new shirt, Durrant."

"Oh pardon me – I didn't fancy a swim just yet."

"I'm terribly sorry, everyone. All OK now," said Duncan.

Giles' punt glided past them. Sylvie patted her raven dyed hair and snapped shut her makeup compact.

"We'd better start looking for a picnic place – perhaps up to the Pleasure, you know, that stretch of grass by the weir."

"Plenty of time, Sylvie. I think this baby could sleep all afternoon."

"She's probably been clubbing all night."

Louisa stuck a thumb in her mouth, her eyes opening briefly.

"Where will you go this summer, Cynthia?" said Sylvie.

"A group of us are going to Italy. Louisa's mother runs a travel company – Two Wheels Good. They do cycling holidays. She's offered to put a trip together for us. We're going to cycle through the Italian countryside and stay in little towns on the way. Bliss. Can't wait. What about you?"

"Rope will have me running the office while he swans off. I do all the recruiting you know, when the little darlings fail their exams and then he comes back without a word of thanks."

Sylvie looked at the prone figure of Ivan.

"Do you think that boy knows what he sounds like?"

"Yo mother, in da doo, yeah, mumumumu, yeah, codunkcadunk, yeah."

Sylvie gestured to Ivan whose head was bobbing to the music being pumped into his head.

"Duncan says that's as near as he gets to an English lesson. He seems harmless now. The rest of the time he gives me the creeps."

Ivan looked up as if he had heard her and Sylvie smiled nervously at him. He stared blankly at her and began to tap out a rhythm on his Armani jeans.

The two punts moved in unison now, each keeping pace with the other. Giles and Duncan negotiated their way around punts filled with Japanese tourists and other punts wildly out of control that drifted across the river to be caught in the branches of trees while their hapless puntsmen failed to respond to the instructions that were shouted at them by their companions. As they rounded a bend in the river, Duncan heard the unmistakable laugh of Mrs Bowler. A punt was lodged against the river bank kept in place by a pole driven into the river bed. Duncan caught sight of Mrs Bowler who was hurriedly buttoning her blouse. The naked torso of Josh appeared from behind her and, for a moment, Duncan thought he had no clothes on at all. He stood up yanking his trouser belt and threading a long tongue of leather into a metal loop on which was embossed a large Confederate flag.

"Fancy seeing you here. Have you got my girl there? Don't let her anywhere near the paddles, wouldn't know which way round to hold them. Ha!"

"Hello, Mrs Bowler. Having a pleasant afternoon?" said Duncan.

"I should say."

Duncan was glad that they had not come across the couple any earlier.

"We're going up to the Pleasure if you want to join us."

"She's already 'ad 'ers." Josh said, smoothing sun tan oil into his arms.

"Thank you, Josh. That'll do. Yes, we'd love to," said Daphne Bowler.

Josh drew their punt alongside Duncan's.

"Right oh mate. I've got the hang of this thing now. Race ya."

With that he set off. Duncan could see that Josh's punting technique left something to be desired and that beating him to the Pleasure would be possible if he could manage to get past him without too many collisions. Giles gestured for Duncan to go forward, rested on his pole and throwing his head back, drained a glass of wine. Duncan assessed the situation. The river divided ahead of him and he now headed for the wider passage keeping a boat's length between him and the competition. As he entered the channel he saw that it was blocked at the other end by a fallen tree. At the same moment Josh swung his punt sideways and Duncan did the same, his bow scraping the side of the other boat as he turned causing Mrs Bowler to fall backwards, kicking her legs in the air.

"Boys, boys."

The two men glared at each other and Duncan nudged Josh's bow with his stern as he went past him so that the opposing punt was propelled into a clump of thorn bushes.

Josh shouted over his shoulder:

"Bloody hell. Nasty little trick."

"Nice one, Captain, nice one."

Steve 'shipped' his paddle, content to watch the combat between these unlikely opponents. Pandora who had been silent and tense up to this point, suddenly came to life and applauded Duncan's manoeuvre.

"Duncan one, the pirate nil! Well done, Duncan."

Duncan, shedding his normal reserve, rolled up his sleeves gave out a whoop and said 'Right, right'. He pointed his craft to the entrance of the narrow channel but before he could reach it Josh had recovered and was beside him. The two punts entered the shaded water together, their gunwales banging against each other as they jostled for position. Josh made a grab for Duncan's pole and the two men were locked in a hand to hand struggle before Duncan managed to throw off his opponent.

"Hurray. Boarders repelled."

"Almost 'ad you that time, Andrew."

"You'll have to try a bit harder than that!"

The lovelies lost interest in their tutor and leaned forward to watch what their Director of Studies would do next.

"Go for it, Mr A."

Duncan peered ahead into the gloom as the punts raced across the water.

He noticed that the river was no more than a wide stream now.

"Keep your hands in, this is going to get tricky."

Pandora, carried away by the excitement of it all kneeled in front of Duncan.

"Ah, my Nelson."

"Steady, Miss Fulbright."

Then he saw his nemesis. Twenty yards ahead the surface of the stream was broken by a solid looking tree trunk. Duncan glanced at Josh who had also seen the obstruction and was having exactly the same thought. The trunk was on the left hand side, if Duncan could edge ahead and force Josh to change sides, then he could clear the stream and emerge the victor in the broad water of the Pleasure now visible in the sunlight.

Josh anticipated this plan and surged forward, the metal tip of his punt pole striking the stony bottom. Neck and neck, they neared the trunk and Duncan in a last desperate attempt to switch positions, rammed the side of the other punt. Rather than dislodging his opponent, this move had the effect of driving Duncan decisively onto the trunk. The punt came to a halt and tilted to the side. Water streamed in along its whole length. Amidst alarmed cries from Pandora, who had now reverted to a state of nervous collapse, Steve moved about the rapidly disappearing duck boards trying to rescue handbags, cameras and valuables, flinging them onto the river bank. Lindsey stood up, throwing off the lovelies.

"I can't swim. I can't swim. Bloody hell."

The punt settled into the water and began a gentle progress into the murky depths. The two lovelies stood up and seemed to be waiting as the water rose up their legs making their summer skirts billow out on the surface, now strewn with the flotsam of their picnic. One of them looked around for somewhere to put her drink as if she had just been asked to dance at a party. A blue cushion floated past her and she placed her glass on its shiny surface.

"Lindsey, aren't you supposed to be rescuing us or something?" said one of the lovelies.

"Yes, Lindsey, what about a bit of gallantry – we're damsels in distress."

"For Christ sake. This isn't funny," said Lindsey.

The water had now reached waist height and even the phlegmatic Steve was beginning to wonder how much deeper they would go. He stood near the lovelies while Lindsey thrashed about grabbing brittle thorn branches that snapped and left him holding handfuls of kindling. By this time Pandora had clamped an arm around Duncan and was gripping him by the wrist.

"My keys, I can't find my keys. How will I get in? Mother. Oh dear, oh dear."

Steve, whose head had been under water for some time, resurfaced, his face hung with bright green algae like a Greek god. He held up a bunch of keys and a pair of sunglasses.

"Whose are these?"

"Thank heavens," said Pandora taking the keys from Steve and thanking him.

"I think it's stopped. Yes, we're on the bottom. I'm dreadfully sorry."

Pandora looked up at Duncan and smiled.

"It wasn't your fault, it was that beastly ..."

"That's very understanding of you, Pandora."

"Dear, oh dear. You're in a bit of a fix. Women and children first?"

Josh had returned without Mrs Bowler. He looked down at the bedraggled group with an expression that was a mixture of mock sympathy and triumphalism. Duncan spoke without looking at him.

"Yes, if you could take the girls and Pandora. Steve and I will try to get the punt up."

By this time Giles had appeared on the bank and took command of proceedings. They had tried to empty the punt from the end but Giles had seen that the best way was to form a line along the side and empty it that way. Having got his manpower in place he gave the command and, with a combination of heaving and sliding, the punt was brought clear of the water. Wading into the stream Duncan retrieved cushions and bags.

*

"That wasn't in the planning, Duncan. What were you doing?"

"Rush of blood to the head, Cynthia. It was that man. No, it was me. Vanity, couldn't stand the thought that this novice would beat me."

"And …?"

"Yes, yes and the younger man. A menopausal moment."

"Good, a bit of self awareness anyway. Well, we certainly won't forget this outing."

The survivors were dotted about on the grass swathed in blankets and sipping at steaming mugs of coffee. The picnic was abandoned and the party broke up. Duncan watched as the other punts returned up river and waited by his doomed craft for the arrival of the punt station motor boat and composed a version of events that would, he hoped, not make him look too foolish.

CHAPTER 6

"Morning, George."

"Ever the early bird, Mr Andrew."

Duncan was relieved to be back at work after the debacle of the outing.

He had decided that the whole event did him little credit but that he seemed to have been forgiven by all concerned. Indeed his vigorous actions, although ill fated seemed to have impressed several people, not the least of whom was Pandora. He had discussed this with Claire who had teased him with warnings about single women of a certain age.

"Good weekend, your honour?"

"It had its moments. Any trouble?"

Duncan always asked this. The proximity of two pubs that had extended opening hours often led to minor damage after the weekend. He had arrived one Monday morning to the sight of three pizzas pinned to the polished surface of the college gate and the remains of several beer bottles carpeting the pavement.

"No, but I do have a surprise for you."

George rubbed his hands together and skipped from side to side.

"Follow me, if you will."

George led Duncan to a yard behind the hostel.

"My bike. George, how did you …?"

"Ah, bit of a story there. I was investigating the contents of one of this fair city's more opulent rubbish bins when I noticed a young fella wheeling your bike along. I knew it was yours straight away so I followed him. Now here was the problem. How to get it back without a ruckus? There was an animal rights demo brewing down the road and as I went I saw four of the fascist bully boys taking a bit of a break. One of them recognized me so I went over and enlisted them. They hung back and I stopped the little rascal – he was all of fifteen but a nasty look in his eye, if you know what I mean. "Oi", says I, "and where did you get that bike from?" Well, straight off he starts effing and blinding at me and protesting his innocence. Says he bought it from a fella in the pub. The question of his underage presence in a pub I left to one side. He then makes various personal remarks about me appearance and station in life and gives me a shove. He gives a scornful scoff when I mention that my friends were close at hand – assuming, I suppose, that they were other gentlemen of the road like myself. My little posse, fully riot geared up they were, had worked their way around behind the boy so that when he turns he's faced by a solid wall of black body armoured no nonsense. It was a treat. "Shit" says the boy, drops the bike and legs it down the road and straight into the arms of the extreme wing of the protect little furry animals mob who do something useful for once and bring the boy back, kicking and screaming, for a bit of corrective treatment from the boys in blue."

"What a result, George. I'm most grateful to you, thank you."

"It's a pleasure. Oh, I'll not be seeing you for a while after today."

"Off on the circuit, George?"

George was one of the few down and outs who still left the city to tramp to Northampton and then to Birmingham to return a month or two later.

"I'll not be long but I feel the need for a bit of travel. My summer holiday you could call it."

Duncan found Peter Rope waiting for him in the college court-yard. He waved an email at him.

"They've been withdrawn."

"Who have?"

"Your crew."

"What?"

"The girls in your punting party. The parents have moved them to Tranters. What were you playing at man?"

"Er, well it was ..."

"You'd better get up there and get a few more hours booked in. Phone some of the Russians. Tell them little Natasha needs more tutorials if she's to get to uniwersity. God, people. Oh, and you might like to sort this out – bit late now but we've got to do it. I'm out for the rest of the day."

The Principal left muttering about nanny states and money. Duncan looked at the thick document he had been given. The cover read: 'Health and Safety-Guidance and Policy Making.'

Chapter 7

The school hall was set out for the Year 12 Parents Evening. At some tables staff were accompanied by nervous looking student teachers, grinning and leafing through mark books, anxious to make some contribution to the conversation that invariably excluded them. The smell of that day's school dinner lingered in the air.

Duncan and Claire Andrew peered at a large board set up in the entrance to the hall and tried to find the location of their daughter's teachers.

"We need a plan. Sarah, come and help us. Do we need to see both teachers or will one do?"

Sarah had two teachers for each of her AS level subjects. Her parents had learned from previous parents' evenings that if they split up they could gather the teachers' comments separately and then compare notes and look for common themes to highlight to their child when they got home.

"I can see the Maths teachers but the others don't seem to be in the right place according to this plan."

Mrs Pike stood by the board. She was dressed in an ill fitting 'power suit', a paper label announcing her name and position as Head of Year 12 stuck to her lapel. She was a tall woman with streaks of grey in her hair and the lined face of a heavy smoker.

"Mr and Mrs Andrew, nice to see you. And how is the lovely Simon?"

Sarah, who had been silent until now, let out an audible 'tsch'.

"He's well, thank you. On his Gap - somewhere in Indonesia."

"He deserves it, he worked very hard, we were very pleased with his results. It was a good year – moved us up the league table nicely."

The laughter that followed indicated that the school's position in the league tables was never in doubt, fed as it was by a gene pool that largely required little more than attendance to ensure healthy exam results.

Mrs Pike turned to Sarah and smiled.

"Hi, Sarah."

"Hi, Miss."

There was a brief pause and Mrs Pike turned back to Sarah's parents.

"Now, how can I help?"

She scanned the hall looking for some order in the mass of people, many of them standing in queues that wove between the desks and lost direction as they intersected with other queues. Good humoured banter audible as parents established to which queue they belonged. Mrs Pike had collected a little posse of Sixth Form helpers around her and she now put an arm around one of them and said:

"Bridie here will tell you where everyone is."

Bridie dressed in regulation Gothic, three lip piercings and military footwear, smiled sweetly at the Andrews and said:

"Follow me, please."

She linked arms with Sarah and led the way. Duncan noted that the sullen demeanor of his daughter was transformed by this gesture and they chatted aimiably as Bridie plunged them into the heaving crowd. He took Claire's hand and followed their guide. After a few twists and turns Duncan managed to position himself beside Bridie and said:

"Remind me what you're doing, Bridie?"

"Double Art and Design Tech. Oh, and Further Maths."

"Interesting choices."

"Yeah, I want to do Aeronautic Design at Uni. Here we are. Mathematics. Oh, and it's better to see both teachers. They all do different modules."

Bridie smiled, her pretty face swathed in hair that had been dyed black with purple streaks. She said 'nice to see you' and shook their hands.

"Nice girl."

"Yeah, but there's no need to chat her up."

"Ah, she speaks! I wasn't chatting her up, just taking an interest."

"Yeah, right."

Duncan saw that the chairs in front of Mr Uglow (Mathematics) were unoccupied and put out his hand to introduce himself. Mr Uglow half rose from his chair and instead of taking Duncan's hand waved his arms and said:

"I'm afraid there are others before you."

Duncan turned to see the stern faces of those at the front of Mr Uglow's queue. Claire touched his arm and said:

"Come on, Sarah's got one of her History teachers."

"Mr and Mrs Andrew. How do you do? Nice to meet you. Have a seat."

Mr Draper extended a clammy hand to them and sat down. He avoided looking at them.

"Now, Sarah. Yes, yes dreadful student. Ha. No, no, only joking. She's, um, she started the course really well. Basically we need to get off that comfy sofa in the common room and get ourselves into class, don't we Sarah?"

The teacher let out a short burst of hysterical laughter. He looked down at his mark book and traced a finger along the register. Duncan noticed that his finger nails and the skin surrounding them had been bitten and chewed, his index and middle finger nicotine stained.

"You've struggled a bit with your Britain paper but your presentation with Ashley on Baldwin was good. Wasn't it Sarah?"

"It was all right. Ashley did most of the work."

"Um, I've got one of your essays here somewhere."

Mr Draper had been covering the marks in his register with his hand, Duncan suspected that this was to disguise the gaps that he knew appeared next to Sarah's name. They waited while the History teacher flicked through a pile of essays, like a bank teller counting notes.

"Yes, here we are. I gave it a D but there are some *really* good passages that you could *really* build on. This paragraph about the Anschluss is *really* good. Basically you just need a bit more depth and the structure needs attention."

Duncan lost interest. This sanitized version of Sarah's performance was no good to them. He looked around the room as students shepherded their parents to the next consultation. At the adjacent table the teacher was delivering a eulogy on the written work of a student whose parents leant forward as if they wanted to remember every word of this reflected glory. They nodded, occasionally patting their offspring on the shoulder as the teacher spoke about the elegance of his student's writing and his quick understanding of historiography. This word produced another round of congratulatory gestures, the parents having no idea what it meant but realizing that it held the possibility of arcane knowledge that would lead on to their son being the first member of their family to go to university. Duncan's attention returned to Mr Draper's attempts at covering his own failure to sound alarm bells about Sarah's increasing indifference to her academic progress. Claire got to her feet:

"Could you call us if Sarah isn't doing what she's supposed to do?"

"Mum!"

"Well, we need to know, Sarah."

Mr Draper wrung his hands together and recognized the early signs of a family row.

"I'm sure it'll all be all right. Less time on the sofa – ha! – and all will be well."

Mr Draper sat down and got up again straight away, the clammy hand with its torn extremities waving at the next parents in the queue.

Dear Aged Ones

Moleskin notebook in my possession and being filled with fascinating travellers information and reflections – days since last visit to toilet, number of blisters on feet, approximate growth rate of beard, consistency of bowel movements when toilet finally required. HEY! I gave you that notebook last Christmas and it was just sitting in your desk drawer!!! Update on Sonny's footwear. The news is not good, following Headman's assurance that Firestone treads were, quote, 'Rolls Royce good for shoes', Sonny is once again shoeless and talking about actually buying a new pair - from the sweat shops of Jakarta when we hit town. Dragons at Dal Lat weird and good. Long tongues. American tourists even weirder. Gee I love your accent etc etc. Has my loan form come thru? Love to all wayward sister included.

Simon

Simon Yoot

Good to hear from you – love the names of the islands, fully expecting you to tell me that you have spent time on Bing Bong next. Now – as well as avoiding Lom Bok you must NOT drink from the bucket. They're full of nasties and, I'm reliably informed, you can catch Hepatitis from just a few sips. While not wishing to curtail any avenues of fun I think the bucket might be one to avoid. Sarah has no doubt e mailed you with lurid details of her latest escapades. We had a gruelling time at parents evening –there seems little hope, a retake year is looming, I suspect. Bit of a change from the paeans you used to get. Can't talk to her at mo. Perhaps you could do a bit of long distance counselling, show her she's not on her own and so on.

Love M and D

CHAPTER 8

STEVE OPENED A BOTTLE of beer and handed it to Duncan. The two friends were sitting in Steve Durrant's attic flat overlooking the Iffley Road Athletic Club. It was early June and the last of the May blossom was fading on the nearby trees. From the flat window the two men could see a group of runners leaning into a bend, their feet pounding over the ground where Bannister and Chataway had made history years before, the cinder track now overlaid by an all weather surface.

It had become a tradition at the college that the Director of Studies and the Classics tutor should be the authors of the DeLouche College end of year review. The first date they put in their diaries at the beginning of the academic year were the two days in June when they would lock themselves away and write the sketches, a mixture of in jokes, parody and what Steve referred to as the high art of piss taking. In accordance with this ritual of creative outpouring, Duncan had arrived the previous afternoon carrying an overnight bag and a ream of blank paper. That evening they had strolled down the road to the Cricketers Arms and discussed the title for the review. Each year they had to come up with a title referring to the word 'rope' in deference to their employer.

"I don't know why we bother."

"He is a man who seems to have had his sense of humour surgically removed at an early age."

"Hey, that's a cracker. We could use that. An operating theatre with students having study habit implants and, and …"

"Save that one for later. What about a title?"

"We can probably recycle some of the early ones now – I always liked On the Ropes."

"What about Money for Old Rope?"

"A bit controversial that – sounds too much like how we earn our living."

"All right : The Bitter End."

"Bit gloomy."

"Not if you understand it."

"Yes, but not everyone has your encyclopedic knowledge of nautical terms."

A stream of University students passed them making their way back to digs on the Iffley Road; they carried bags of shopping in each hand, backpacks with the days work slung on their shoulders. Duncan watched a girl on her bike, her summer skirt tucked under her seat, coming towards them.

"We get older, they never do. One of the penalties of living in a university town: the constant reminder of one's mortality."

"Now that really is gloomy."

They pushed the pub door open and walked past the little performance area that was used for live music nights. There was a poster near the entrance that announced: 'Steve Durrant and the Isis Band play Kenny Barron'.

"Tomorrow night's gig?"

"Yeah, the best sort. I can play all night and then just roll home to bed."

They ordered two pints of Hook Norton and bought a box of panatella cigars. This, too, was part of the ritual. Duncan was much more used to drinking wine these days and had given up smoking but they had acquired superstitions that helped them when faced with the blank page and the need to come up with enough material to fill the hour long review. The panatellas were added after a particularly fruitful evening in Steve's flat when they had written a sketch that involved a stuffed camel, fifteen girls dressed in grass skirts and a traffic warden with a talent for snake charming. Neither Steve nor Duncan could remember why this was funny but it had been rapturously received and so pints of Hookie and cigars had been added to the neurosis of writing.

"Here's an idea. We do a sketch about terrorists."

"On the principle that if we didn't laugh we'd cry?"

"Exactly."

"Go on."

"OK. There are two groups – the Oswestry Liberation Army and the Movement for Suffering Sufis, for example – and they are given a safe house, except it's the same safe house and they have to share it. And one group hath a thpeech impediment."

" Derivative, but that's never stopped us before. Conflicting ideologies, having to sleep facing Birmingham, promises of fourteen virgins from Newcastle to add a touch of irony. Excellent. Offensive, of course, but containing distinct comedic possibilities."

" How very odd," said Duncan.

"The odder the better," Steve drained his pint.

"No. Look."

Both men saw Lindsey North on the pavement opposite the pub. He was speaking to two people that Duncan recognized as Colonel Smirka and his secretary.

"My, she's a looker. North plying his evil trade as usual. Mind you, I wouldn't fancy his chances against that bloke."

Duncan noticed that Colonel Smirka and Lindsey were speaking to each other without the aid of the secretary.

"I didn't know Lindsey could speak Russian," said Duncan.

"Perhaps they're speaking in English."

Duncan knew this was not possible. He saw Lindsey and Colonel Smirka shaking hands and turn away from each other. Lindsey had taken no notice of the secretary. Duncan rose to his feet and moved towards the bar with their empty glasses.

After their third pint – no more, no less each year – they wandered down Circus Street and onto the Cowley Road in search of a takeaway. Duncan, unused to the beer and cigars was feeling light headed and out of place. A Big Issue seller in combat trousers and a beanie in the colours of the Jamaican flag stopped them and they bought a copy, dropping it in the nearest waste bin. Steve hailed a man whose dreadlocks reached down to his shoulders.

"Respect."

"Respect."

"Working?"

The man nodded and looked up at a window above a shop advertising Moldavian Cuisine. He turned to Steve and said in a sing song Caribbean voice:

"One of the clients is chuckin' water at passers-by. I'm jus waitin' for him to do it again. Then I'll go and have a word before the Babylon arrive."

Duncan looked up and could see the silhouette of a teenage boy through an open window. They moved on.

"Who was that?"

"Nattie, he houses young offenders and then looks after them, keeps them out of trouble. He drums for me sometimes."

They ordered their food and sat in the window of an Indian Takeaway eating handfuls of Bombay mix.

"Shouldn't eat this really. They analysed a handful once and found…"

"Enough information. I need some – to soak up the beer. I'm not used to it."

An old woman stood on the pavement opposite them and looked up and down the road. Her hands gripped the frame of a shopping trolley, the tartan pattern of the basket frayed and stained. A girl stopped and took her by the arm and guided her across the road.

"Small acts," said Steve.

"Makes the world go round."

They watched people coming and going and the traffic moving slowly towards the city centre.

"You OK?" said Duncan.

"Never better. We're playing most weekends now and I'm trying to persuade the band to do the Truck Fest. this year. I won't be able to give up the day job but we make a bit of cash. Takes me out of myself. Blowing. It's good. You?"

"Fine. Spot of bother with the youngest but otherwise clear skies."

"Adolescence, eh? I can cope with it one to one in tutorials but being a parent – no thank you."

"It's not that bad. Rough patches, good patches."

"You've another life. Insurance policy for your old age. I've never fancied it."

"Even without children? You know, just a partner?"

"No. Wouldn't do me. Used to me own ways," said Steve.

"I'm not sure what my own ways are," said Duncan.

"Ah, ha. Do I detect a note of regret from the married family man?"

A scarlet jacketed waiter appeared and held up two brown paper bags.

"One chicken tikka, one lamb passanda, bindibarji, pilau rice and two nan. Enjoy your meal, Mr Steve."

"Ta. Come on mate, time to trough."

CHAPTER 9

DARK SHADOWS MOVED ACROSS the walls of his room. Somewhere a car door slammed. He listened for any other sound but could only hear muffled laughter coming from the TV two floors below his room. He knew his mother would be watching her favourite programme, an imitation of a British game show, and would not move until it finished. He listened again. A dog barked in the street below his window. He wondered if he had had enough, or if he would come again. He felt for his boxer shorts and pulled them on, moving his duvet to cover his body. He listened for the sequence of noises that would announce his return. The door handle at the bottom of the stairs being turned, thirteen footfalls, a creak on the seventh step, and then the door handle into his room slowly turning. He stared wide eyed at the wall, afraid that even if he blinked he would not hear the first sound.

PART 2

CHAPTER 10

The Two Wheels Good cycling party sat back on their saddles and took in the view. They had been pedalling along a back road leading through fields of blue rape and tall stands of maize that crackled in the warm sun. The road had meandered over gentle undulations making the cycling effortless and, apart from one Fiat van labouring along with bales of straw towering above the driver's cabin, their route had been uninterrupted by any vehicles. They rode spread out across the road, Lindsey showing off by riding with his arms folded, a movement that Cynthia Digit had copied to the cheers of the others in the party. There had been little conversation between them and none at all as they leant into the last gradient, the click, click antiphony of gear shift accompanying the change of terrain. Before them lay a shallow valley alive with the sound of cicadas and, at its centre, the land gathered into a peak on top of which was a village, its weathered walls making it hard to distinguish between the manmade and the rock on which it had been built. The outcrops that supported the buildings made a mass of jagged surfaces and seemed at odds with the silky landscape that lay all around.

"Look, sunflowers. A whole field of them."

Louisa dismounted, letting her bike fall to the road. She walked over rutted ground past wrecked stalks of sunflowers, their heads burnt and wasted by the sun, until she reached an area where the banal flowers were still golden yellow. She ran her hand over one of the ribbed stems, feeling the sharp resistance of its fibrous surface and watched as a vermillion coloured beetle made its way across the honeycombed disk of the flower head. When she returned to the road the others were resting on the verge passing bottled water between themselves in what had become a familiar ritual of their wayside breaks.

"This'll do. This – will – do," said Steve lying back on a grassy bank.

Pandora Fulbright, unable to take her eyes off the perfection before her, squinted through the view finder on her camera and moved it back and forth. Trees, the road, empty barns and telegraph poles blurred through the segmented square until she had found the right combination of field and cypress tree and farmhouse, its terracotta walls matching exactly the pictures she had seen in postcards and brochures. She took other photos and added them in her mind to the photo diary she would show her mother on her return. Mrs Fulbright would sit in the arm chair with the antimacassar and peer at the bulging images through her magnifying glass and make cooing noises to indicate her interest as her daughter explained each picture. Her mother would want to know all about her trip, as she had always done when her daughter had gone to places beyond her known, suburban world. Pandora folded her camera back into its case and shading her eyes with her hand began to take mental photos, storing them away as a bulwark against the coming drizzle of an English winter.

Daphne Bowler unclipped the map holder from the handle bars of her bike and smoothed its clear plastic surface. The Touring

Club Italiano No 661 map had been folded to show the route they had taken that day and their destination was marked with a red circle. Daphne was pleased with their progress, no-one had fallen behind and there had been little grumbling when they had ended their breaks and resumed the serious business of 'getting on'. In the early days of the company she had lost some repeat business by being too overtly keen to reach the daily mileage objectives, objectives driven by the need to arrive at their bookings in time for the evening meal. She was now practised at moving her clients on without making them feel they were being dragooned into action. She looked at Steve's recumbent figure and congratulated herself at maintaining the illusion of relaxed progress.

"Well leader, are we where we should be?"

"Spot on, Andrew. You see before you the village of Bastardo and somewhere in there the Villa Mia and a funghi tagliatelli that will not disappoint."

The sky erupted with the deafening sound of jet engines and two fighter planes of the Italian Air Force dropped into the valley and then banked away and disappeared over the low hill at its eastern end. Pandora covered her ears and hopped anxiously from foot to foot and said 'horrid, horrid' although no-one could hear her. The planes had made them all get to their feet and for a moment they stared in the direction of the vanished aircraft as the day closed behind them and the silenced cicadas resumed their chafing. The little party performed a pantomime of movement, doing up zips; putting items back into the multi-coloured day bags provided by the company; bending to fold trouser legs back into socks. The cyclists remounted and free wheeled down the hill towards a bend in the road leading to Bastardo.

CHAPTER 11

THE BAR IN THE Villa Mia was festooned in the yellow and black colours of Juventus Football Club and between a row of optics, colour portraits of the 1985 team had been bluetacked to the wall. A replica of the three European cups they had won that year were the centre piece of a chrome shelf crowded with rosettes and local trophies. At one end of the bar was a much older picture showing the village piazza in faded sepia with two military trucks in the foreground and a group of uniformed men lined up and grinning at the camera. A rectangular label had been stuck to the oak frame of the picture: Brigade Militare di Bastardo 1942. Above the bar a wide screen television was showing a football match, the rumble and rhythm of the commentator and crowd mirroring the proximity or distance of the players to the goal areas. The bar was empty except for a dozing Alsatian lying under the bead screen that filled the open doorway of the bar and filtered the early evening sunlight making the interior pleasantly cool. Pandora Fulbright and Louisa Bowler sat beside each other on a bench outside the bar. They were writing postcards and had raised their feet on tip toe to rest the cards on their knees while they wrote, each pausing occasionally to look up before bowing their heads again to resume writing. Louisa was writing to one of her school friends and the words KNACKERED and BORING and PISSED appeared in the middle of sentences written in bold print. Along one side of the card she had drawn a sunflower and a stick man version of herself standing beside it. The sun- flower was as tall as herself. Next to her Pandora crafted each sentence to convey as much of the day's delights as she could manage and then signed the card Love Pan xxx

"I think we have company."

Pandora indicated down the cobbled street to a group of young people, the boys in combat trousers and tee shirts, the girls in shorts and camisoles. They streamed past Pandora and Louisa in a blur of laughter as they tripped over the Alsatian who yelped and moved out of their way. The beaded curtain jumped and rattled as they poured through the entrance. Louisa followed them, relieved to have come across some other young people. She tried to recognize the languages they were speaking but then realized that they were speaking English as well as their own.

"Hi, my name is Stanislaw. This is my sister Peta. We are from Estonia." Louisa became the centre of attention as they all introduced themselves and announced their nationalities – German and Swedish and Croatian and one girl with streaming red hair from Luxembourg.

"What are you all doing here?"

Peta was making bunches of her blonde hair and winding them into hair bands.

"Travelling around."

This seemed infinitely romantic to Louisa who was already tired of her Mother's hectoring and the sheer age of the others. Admittedly Lindsey was younger but she had seen him leering at girls in the street and decided that he was creepy.

"Cool."

"We stay at the Youth Hostel, over there."

Stanislaw waved a hand in the general direction of battlements that were threaded through the village and that included fortified towers one of which had been converted into a youth hostel.

"We are on bicycles."

Louisa said this as if it were in some way a little shameful but Stanislaw thought this, too, was 'cool' and asked her where they had come from that day. A boy with a shock of peroxide hair leant over the bar and called for service. There was a good natured shout from somewhere behind the bar and the proprietor appeared wiping his hands on a tea towel emblazoned with the Juventus crest and miniature images of each member of the current team. Holding four glasses in one hand he flicked a china tap and filled them with lager. Raising his chin in the direction of a bowl full of pistachio nuts, he instructed the peroxide boy to distribute these in smaller containers. The boy had taken a moment to follow what the man was saying and then had repeated 'Si' several times to indicate his understanding and to show that he knew at least one Italian word. As the Villa Mia bar came to life, the Two Wheels Good party arrived from their rooms, showered and fragrant and ready for their first drink. The noise level rose exponentially and space at the bar and on tables was made for the new arrivals. A Babel of names from England to the far Eastern reaches of Europe accompanied by furious hand shaking and raised glasses rose into the air. Louisa felt a little betrayed that her new friends mingled happily with the middle aged group and seemed not to notice how old and dull they were. The proprietor, grinning broadly and producing a conveyor belt of brimming glasses, shouted his greetings to the new arrivals and took no notice of their requests for wine and soft drinks. Lager, it seemed, was all that was on offer and the guests accepted it with equally broad grins. The absence of locals released any inhibitions they might have felt and young and not so young took noisy and joyous possession of this place. Duncan spoke to their host.

"Dove sono gli altri? The people who live here?"

"Se ne sono andati. Al paese vicino. Calcio. Oggi."

"Quale ?"

"Norcia."

Duncan was unsure if this meant that the proprietor felt sick when he thought about the neighbouring village or whether this was its name. He hoped it was the latter – the prospect of a match between Bastardo and Norcia was particularly delicious and an ideal opportunity for laughing at foreigners, a habit he had not managed to kick even in these days when such things were frowned upon. Duncan barked another sentence at the proprietor (which started with 'Quelli che' but he couldn't think of the word for win) when the burly Italian thrust a heavy glass tankard full of lager at Duncan's head. Duncan ducked the blow, prepared to parry the next thrust and wondered what dreadful mistake he had made with his Italian that had changed this genial man into a Neapolitan street fighter.

"Padre."

A pudgy, white fist appeared over Duncan's shoulder and gripped the tankard.

"Mille grazie."

Duncan turned to see the rubicund face of Bastardo's village priest, Father Dromo. Wishing Duncan 'Buonasera' he drained his glass in one go and demanded a refill. The padre smiled out of myopic eyes framed by circular lenses and placed at a jaunty angle on his red face, the bridge of his glasses long since broken and held together by a graying piece of elastoplast. Gripping his refilled glass he grinned at Duncan and said "Manu, Naucasle, Arsinale" and sent the litre of golden liquid in the same direction as the first.

"Steve, I think you may have met your match here."

Steve Durrant was surrounded by four young Swedes who were discussing the relative merits of Swedish and English cuisine, Steve had temporarily stunned them by referring to 'faggots and mushy peas' as the food of the gods.

"What's that?" said Steve.

"The good father here. Downing them in one."

"Good man."

Steve turned back to his companions who had now gathered their wits and put forward the case for Lutfisk, Kroppkakor and Inlagd Sill all of which, Steve thought, sounded like skin disorders. Undeterred, he fought back with tripe, deadman's leg and jellied eels. It was going to be a long evening.

Father Dromo now surveyed the clientele, looked at his watch and spoke to his fellow countryman. Duncan picked out the words 'ospite' and 'ospitalita' and assumed that the next stop for the priest was the local hospital.   Brushing cigarette ash from his cassock, the priest tapped the side of his nose and winked at Duncan. Unsure how to respond to this he said with triumphant irrelevance "Absolutely" at which Father Dromo chucked him affectionately under the chin and left accompanied by the dog who had had quite enough of the noise and was off to find somewhere quieter to spend the evening.

Louisa was sitting at a table with the brother and sister from Estonia.

"We play music. Peta and I. We come from Tallin."

Louisa had a vague idea that Estonia was near Russia but she had never heard of Tallin.

"It is our capital city. Very beautiful. You must visit."

Louisa smiled, the possibility of her travelling to a country in Eastern Europe being too remote to contemplate.

"Great, great. What kind of music do you play."

"We like acoustic rock. We listen to Radio Blast at home all the time."

"Radio Blast?"

"It plays music we like; Fairport Convention, The Albion Band, Steel Eye Span. Once we went in and played some of our compositions."

"Cool. I go to clubs in London. At the weekends. The Moon Club something "

"It must be great. So many clubs. We know about the Half Moon in Putney."

"Yes. I was there. I went to hear John Renbourn. He was really old but he played some amazing stuff."

Stanislaw and Peta intoned the musician's name and looked at Louisa in awe.

"Oh, Renbourn he is fantastic. We have all his records. And Bert Jansch."

Peta and Stanislaw stared at Louisa and waited for her to go on. She was not used to this. Most of what she said was either ignored or dismissed as incorrect or irrelevant by her mother and her school mates. Because of this she had fallen into the habit of speaking in a kind of ambiguous short hand, but here were two people who actually wanted to hear what she had to say.

"Well. I live in North London. So I get the underground from the Angel and get off at Piccadilly and walk up through Soho till I get to Greek Street. The Edge Club is in a tiny basement room. It's great. Last time I heard Ralph McTell. When you come to London I'll show you around."

Louisa rummaged in her shoulder bag and produced a battered Pocahontas pencil case. She wrote down her address and telephone number on a paper napkin and gave it to her new friends.

Daphne Bowler sat with her back to Louisa and next to a young man who was rolling up his sleeve and showing her a series of scars that ran the length of his arm.

"I thought that was the stuff of legend," she said.

Daphne ran her fingers along the length of his arm feeling its muscular strength and regretted that she had dispensed with Josh whose only crime had been that he had not been prepared to be at her beck and call. She had a sudden memory of Josh's body moving above her in the punt on the Cherwell and felt the old, urgent need rising in her.

"In Heidelberg we like to keep the old tradition going, but quietly."

"How wonderful, do you have duels at night by torchlight?" Daphne purred.

"Yes, swirling cloaks and all," said the young German.

"You must have to keep fit."

"Oh, yes, I am very fit."

"I certainly wouldn't disagree with that," said Daphne.

Darkness had now fallen in the deserted piazza. Louisa sat on the bench where she had written her postcard. She had seen her mother pawing at the German boy and didn't want to be in the same room as her. The piazza was lit by the swan necked lampposts they had seen in every other 'commune' on their route. Louisa fiddled with her nose and wondered why her mother had to spoil all her good times. This thought was interrupted by the appearance of a juke box moving across the piazza, apparently under its own steam. Louisa blinked and saw the bell like shape of Father Dromo's cassock behind the moving object. He was pushing the juke box over the cobbled surface. It swung from side to side and was only prevented from falling over by the priest who danced around the machine shoving and heaving at its chrome sides. He was occasionally caught up in the flex that trailed and bounced behind it like the tail of some improbable beast. The fan shaped hood that contained the playing mechanism caught the light from the street lamps and seemed to light up as if it could not wait for the surge of electricity and the tapping of buttons that would activate the metal arm and deliver a vinyl disk to the turntable. Man and machine continued their erratic progress across the piazza until Father Dromo attempted a particularly dexterous manoeuvre. He tripped over the hem of his cassock, tried unsuccessfully to grasp the flailing lead in a desperate attempt to arrest the progress of the machine and was left sprawling on the ground. The juke box now accelerated over the sloping ground sending sparks into the night air as it veered from side to side. Father Dromo sat up and bellowed a warning to anyone who might be in the path of the rogue juke box:

"Mamma mia. Achtung. Attenzione."

The shallow carriage on which the juke box was mounted came to an abrupt halt against the kerb outside the bar causing it to shoot forward across the pavement and, by a stroke of divine intervention, rocket through the doorway sending the beaded curtain dancing in every direction and coming to a halt just before hitting the chair on which the thoroughly alarmed Pandora Fulbright was sitting. The babble of conversation stopped. There was a moment of surprised silence at which point Father Dromo appeared at the doorway, his ruddy face beaming as he passed a lace edged handkerchief over his bald and sweating brow. There was an uproar of applause and he was lifted briefly into the air by the young Swedes who slapped him on the back and shook his hand as if he had just completed some feat of athletic or sporting excellence which, in a way, he had.

"Per favore. Grazie. Per piacere. Grazie, grazie."

The installation of the juke box complete, Father Dromo set about disabling the payment mechanism. He leaned over the convex surface of the machine, so that his face was made seraphic by the light and selected five records. The heavy and familiar chords of 'Pinball Wizard' filled the little room and triggered another cheer. Lindsey took advantage of this moment of euphoria to put his arm around the flame haired girl from Luxembourg who had by then had so much to drink that she did not object. Duncan squeezed past Steve Durrant who had come to the end of his culinary repertoire and was moving away from the peroxide Swede who was shouting 'Falukorv' at him.

"What's he saying?"

"It might be a Swedish delicacy or he might be telling you to fuck off – hard to tell really. The Padre's done us proud," said Steve.

" Yes, I thought he was off on his hospital rounds. Must have changed his mind," said Duncan.

Steve and Duncan spotted Cynthia who was sitting on a table with a girl who appeared to be crying.

"Eh up. Cynthia's gone into housemother mode. She needs rescuing."

The girl, who was from Bordeaux had been telling Cynthia about her parents and their divorce. She wiped her eyes and smiled at the two men when they sat down. Duncan thought that her Pre-Raphaelite good looks were slightly spoilt by her triple nose piercings but her youth and vulnerability produced a surge of paternal feelings in him.

"This is Mimi. She's been telling me about her parents."

"Pardon my tears but it is a sad time for me."

"Now then, no apologies. Whatever your parents are up to mustn't be allowed to spoil your holiday. Besides, you mustn't disappoint the Padre after he risked life and limb to bring us entertainment."

"Life and limb?"

"Un passage dangeroux pour notre felicite."

Van Morrison was singing 'Spanish Rose' and Louisa had joined a little group who were engaged in an obscure pub game that involved touching noses and clapping hands in a particular sequence, the completion of which produced an outburst of applause. When 'Yellow Submarine' came on everyone joined in, it was not as grand as Beethoven's anthem for Europe but seemed to affirm this microcosm of the Community. Duncan raised his glass to Daphne Bowler and mouthed 'thank you' to her. The last sequence of records came to end with Abba belting out 'Waterloo' and Father Dromo waved his arms for silence.

"Allora. Cantate. You sing now."

Chairs were thrust back and commands shouted across the tables. There was a chaos of movement as the room rearranged itself along national lines. When these manoeuvres had been completed Father Dromo invited the Germans to begin. There was a hurried consultation and then three girls clapped and hummed the introduction to Ode to Joy and the graduate from Heidelberg began in sonorous tones:

"O Freunde, nicht diese Tone!

Sondern latuns angenehmere anstimmn.

Und freudenvollere!"

The girls held their hands over their chests and came in on cue echoing the male voice:

"Freude

Freude

Schooner Gotterfunken,

Tochter aus Elysium

Wir betreten feuertrunken ..."

The rapturous applause that greeted their performance was followed by furious consultations in each group as they decided on what they would sing. It was clear that national pride was now at stake. The United Kingdom appeared to be in a state of disarray as Steve's suggestion of On Ilkley Moor Baht Aht was rejected and CampDown Races dismissed as American.

"What about Clementine?"

"Isn't that Irish? Anyway we won't know all the words."

"God save the Queen?"

"No. Too obvious. Look, if the worst comes to the worst we can give them Rule Britannia?"

"Too nationalist. Listening to Waterloo was bad enough."

Pandora had been silent during this discussion but now showed uncharacteristic firmness by telling them to leave it to her. She would sing.

"Well if you're sure. What will it be?"

"Wait and see."

Peta and Stanislaw wove their way to the centre of the room and said that they were going to sing an Estonian folk song that told the story of seven little elves who rescue the bewitched beautiful Grecia. Their trained voices delighted the audience and this too was received with approval and led to another round of drinks. The proprietor was helped by Mimi and Louisa who were behind the bar washing empties. The massed choir of the Swedes came next. They had produced a duvet cover in the yellow and blue of the Swedish flag and draped it over their shoulders as they sang the curiously disjointed sounds of their national anthem.

"Du gamla, due fria, du fjallhoga Nord

Du tysta, du gladjerika skona!

Jag halso dig, vanaste land uppa jord

Din sol, din himmel, dina angder grona

Dinsol, din hjimmel dina angder groan"

The singing moved on from Lithuanian to Belgian to Luxembourg and then France was called upon to sing. Mimi stepped forward. She slapped her tea towel over her shoulder and climbed onto the bar. She sang Edith Piaf, and, like Piaf, the resonance of her voice coming from a slim body had the same ability to hold an audience enthralled; when she reached the predictable finale tears streamed down her face and every heart went out to her.

"No, rien de rien

No je ne regrette rien"

"Follow that," Steve said ruefully to Pandora.

"I'll try."

The mood in the room had swung from raucous enjoyment, to sentimentality to a serious appreciation of the quality of some of the singing and it seemed that no more emotions were possible. They were drained and tired but wanted to hold onto this moment and Pandora provided them with something that allowed them to do just that. She started haltingly, coughed and stopped. It was not a deliberate ploy to build expectation but it had the same effect.

"Youth gone and beauty gone if ever there

Dwelt beauty in so poor a face as this:

Youth gone and beauty gone what remains of bliss?

I will not bind fresh roses in my hair

Leave youth his roses, who can bear a thorn-

I will not seek for blossoms anywhere

Except such common flowers as blow with corn"

Every face was turned towards Pandora, like blooms seeking sunlight. She paused and drew breath, her eyes fixed on a vanished point above her audience's heads.

"Youth gone and beauty gone, what doth remain?

The longing of a heart pent up forlorn

The silence of a heart that sings its songs

While youth and beauty made a summer morn,

Silence of love that cannot sing again."

More tears shed, the drink and the human voice having an equal impact. The quiet applause after Pandora's last line gave way to silence. Father Dromo let it settle in the room and then gently thanked all of those who had sung and spoke about the power of communion. He spoke to them in Italian but they all understood him. The tranquility of the moment was shattered by the arrival of the Bastardo football team and their supporters. The match had been a close run thing but in the end Bastardo had prevailed. The Captain was carried shoulder high to the bar where he placed the new trophy next to the others. They had brought it home and could not have been more pleased. The recent arrivals were absorbed into the party and locals and foreigner alike joined in the celebrations which went on until dawn.

CHAPTER 12

THE BELLS OF THE Campinale Maggiore faded into silence, the leather harnesses creaking as they came to rest. A flight of pigeons circled the tower and flew away across the hilltop town of San Verino. Shutters were opened and water splashed across the pavement carrying the dust and detritus of the afternoon into cobbled gutters and away through ancient drain covers. A waiter in the Café Garibaldi smoothed the white front of his apron and moved among the al fresco tables placing a bougainvillea blossom on each of them. On the other side of the square Signor Bignole sat at his ornate table in the reception of the Hotel Al Sole. He was glad to be out of the fierce sunlight that, even in the late afternoon, was causing women to fan their faces and men to remove their linen jackets and walk with them slung over their shoulders. Pressing a button marked 'entrada' plate glass doors slid open carrying the ornately engraved letters AS through thin air on reflected light. This piece of electronic magic always pleased Signor Bignole. He had retained the heavy sandalwood doors of the original Albergo and employed someone to polish the brass door studs and the huge dolphin door knockers. These ancient doors were never closed in the long summer season but made a satisfying counterpoint to the modernity of the automatic glass doors whose reassuring swish as they withdrew between long, nylon lips always gave the proprietor the feeling that all was well with the world. Signor Bignole sifted through a pile of receipts and rang a little bell.

"Lucia, I cannot read your writing on these bills."

Lucia was Signor Bignole's niece whom he had hired as a favour to his brother. She had dropped out of university and narrowly avoided a prison sentence when it was discovered that her lover, a young anarchist with ambition, had planned to assassinate a prominent member of the current government.

Lucia appeared in the reception doorway, her mass of raven black hair piled above her slim neck. She looked past her uncle to the sunlit forecourt beyond the entrance to the hotel.

"When the English party arrive you will be here?"

"Yes, Uncle."

"They have come a long way today."

Lucia was not listening, but looked briefly at her uncle.

"From Bastardo."

Lucia folded her arms, sighed and looked again at the empty forecourt.

"They will need to be welcomed and shown to their rooms."

"Yes, Uncle."

Signor Bignole had little faith in Lucia carrying out these duties with any grace but knew that her dark good looks and long legs would offset any lack of courtesy that might be felt, by the men at least.

The distinctive sound of a Fiat Cinquecento engine struggling up
the slope that led to the hotel had an electrifying effect on Lucia.
As the sunlight fell on Lucia's retreating figure she withdrew a silver hair grip holding her hair in place and moved towards the tiny
mustard yellow vehicle, its curved surfaces at odds with the sleek
lines of Audis and BMWs dotted around the square. A young
man uncurled himself from the car like a snake uncoiling from
its basket. It seemed impossible that such a tall figure could have
emerged from the diminutive car. He leaned an elbow on the
Fiat's roof and lit a cigarette.

"Don't be late, Lucia."

"No, Uncle."

Lucia kissed the young man on both cheeks and he wound himself back into the driver's seat. The engine wheezed into life and
they were gone.

Duncan Andrew stood in the shower cubicle and let fine jets of
water play over his tired body. The DeLouche cycling party had
ridden a comfortable twenty kilometres through pleasantly undu-
lating countryside and arrived more or less together at the Hotel
Al Sole fulfilling the schedule for the day set by Two Wheels
Good with an hour or two to spare. Duncan closed his eyes and
let the images of the afternoon replay: roadside crucifixes; stands
of pencil thin cypresses marking the drive to hazy hilltop farm-
houses; closed villages; stopping to cross a motorway, the drone of
brightly coloured goodstrucks moving north to Milan and Zurich,
into the heart of Europe. Duncan had always been struck by this
proximity of nations and the weight of history that went with it.
As he stared up at the drivers he was excited by the thought that
within hours they would have emerged from well lit tunnels to
wait at traffic lights where road signs point to three or four different countries and place names change within a hundred yards

of each other on the way to Vienna or Budapest or Prague. His island mentality continued to enjoy the strangeness of this as he reached for a lemon coloured bar of soap working it between his hands and applying it to the soft surface of his chest. His shower washing proceeded automatically and predictably: having dealt with his front, the burgeoning man breasts and swelling stomach, an inevitable consequence of the aging process which even regular visits to the gym could not counteract; he then resoaped and lifted his left leg to rest his ankle on his right knee. From this position he could run his fingers between his toes and along the calloused underside of his foot. Reversing this movement he cleaned his right foot and moved on to his calves and thighs. Next, he waved his hands back and forth over his back, his fingers moving gently over an elongated scar that ran vertically up his back, the result of a lamenectomy when he was eighteen. He felt the small indentations where the stitches had been anchored but avoided the purple track of the scar itself. With each part of his body came a mental inventory, an assessment of his rate of degeneration. His legs, he was pleased to note, seemed to be holding up well and still had the muscular solidity of his youth, but the folds of flesh developing around his triceps were an uncomfortable reminder of his mortality. He had noted this loosening of the flesh in his father as he got older and now here he was going the same way. Duncan attacked the soap bar as if he wanted to wash this thought away and then set about his testicles and penis. Since watching a Channel Four programme on testicular cancer he had lingered over his scrotum and felt for any lumps or irregularities. All seemed to be well. He had told Simon about the programme just before his departure for Indonesia and advised him to do the same and had felt pleased with himself for having broached such a personal subject with an air of openness. This self congratulation was marred by his knowledge that he had failed completely to help his son through his emerging adolescent sexual awareness. Claire had encouraged him to talk to fifteen year old Simon about sex and Duncan had said that he would but never had. Duncan replaced the soap in the little wire cage fitted to the corner of the shower and lifted a sachet of shampoo into the palm of his hand. He tried to tear a corner of the sachet but it was too slippery and so he bit it instead. Spitting out a jet of bitter tasting liquid, he held the sachet over his head and squeezed. The inventory of decline had now reached the most painful item. It was possible to disguise most of the signs of middle age with clothes but the hair, or the loss of it, marked you out as being over the hill. Duncan had always had a receding hair line, even as a young man but these inlets of hairless scalp had now spread inland leaving the crown of his head populated by marshy tufts. These days Duncan spent very little time massaging the top of his head before moving to the more profuse areas at the back. The routine now complete, Duncan stood with his head bent watching as streams of white foam coursed over his stomach and filled the shower tray with a maelstrom of eddies before draining away.

He padded around his room swathed in an enormous white towel and tried to feel the liberation of the family man released from his daily chores and able to be as he pleased. Pushing open his window he peered down at the Café Garibaldi and decided that he would have a beer before the rest of the party gathered for dinner. This act of self determination, unfettered by the need to wait for Claire or worry about what the children would do should have felt delicious, instead he just felt a little bereft, a little mean and disloyal. Duncan rolled deodorant under both arms and across his chest in a parody of benediction 'testicles, spectacles, wallet and pouch'. Simon and Sarah had always giggled at this irreverence as their father made his final checks before leaving the house in the morning. Claire always tutted at this vulgarity but this made the moment even more enjoyable, its innocent naughtiness a part of the complex bond between them. Duncan ran a comb through the beginnings of a holiday beard. It was no more than stubble but indicated a distancing from his life at home. He selected a pair of blue linen trousers and a pink shirt from his temporary wardrobe and, as a final act of going native, slipped his shoes on without socks. Duncan was not a naturally vain man but age had made him pay more attention to his appearance. He thought about the Irish girl in the cappuccino kiosk and wondered if this was at the bottom of his desire to appear at his best. Shrugging his shoulders he took a final glance in the mirror and, remembering that there was no fool like an old fool, he made his way to the bar.

Pandora Fulbright was pleased with the postcards she had bought in the little supermarket where the DeLouche cycling party had stopped to buy lunch. She had bought ten cards, one for each day they were to be away, and ten stamps so that all she would need to find every morning was a post box. She wondered how long they would take to reach England and imagined Tariq, their postman, opening the garden gate to deliver them. She spread them out on her bed and looked at each one in turn. The little rectangles of light and colour were lovely and all the more so, she thought, for being the places she had passed through that day. She selected a card that was divided into nine squares. Each square had a close up of a 'typical' image – shuttered windows on a terra cottta wall, a lambretta, an ornate street lamp, pots of geraniums on a weathered doorstep. She knew that her mother would not have seen these manufactured clichés as anything other than pictures from another planet. Pandora had not been abroad for years but as a young woman she had travelled through Europe and North Africa and sent her parents news from places they had never visited, preferring instead to sit in deck chairs in Lytham and Grange-over-Sands and once, in a moment of adventure, Cromer. Pandora remembered these holidays as the last of the afternoon sun burned ochre and purple in the Italian sky. As a girl she had walked along windswept promenades and sat with blankets over her knees listening to brass bands while her parents tapped their feet. Later, she would be sent out to get fish and chips to bring back to the stuccoed boarding house where they were staying. Once, she stopped on a bench and a boy asked if he could have a chip. She held out the bag and when he took a chip he leaned towards her and kissed her. Pandora looked back at the double bed and it seemed to be an accusation, to underline her failure as a woman and this forty year old memory burned in her as if it had happened yesterday. She turned back to her postcard and began to write. She knew that her mother's eyesight would not have been up to reading the card but crammed as much writing as possible in the space. When she finished she glanced at her watch and saw that she had a little time before joining the others. Lying on the bed she stared at the ceiling and listened to the sounds of the passagata in the street below her window.

Cynthia Digit sat at the little ornate dressing table in her hotel bedroom and pinched a cleansing pad out of its packet. She raised her chin and ran her fingers along her neck smoothing away the horizontal lines and creases that were etched into her skin. Looking at her pale face in the mirror she drew the white pad across her forehead and over the bridge of her nose. Selecting another pad she wiped her cheeks and the narrow area under her lips. Gathering her thick hair into a pony tail she twisted an elastic band until her hair was held firmly away from her face. Dipping her fingers into a small box she unwrapped a cube of chocolate. This was a local speciality that Cynthia had remembered from years ago when she and Doug had hitchhiked through the area. Giafettis were irresistible. Cynthia held the confectionery up so that she could see its stratified layers. The surface was pure dark chocolate, underneath were three layers of wafer soaked in alcohol and beneath that a fudge that had an explosive impact on the senses. Cynthia remembered how she and Doug had lain naked together feeding each other giafettis as a prelude to making love in hotel rooms not dissimilar to the one she now occupied and the memory of it made her smile. She remembered reading somewhere that the connection between chocolate and sex was not coincidental, that chocolate had some property that released a pleasure hormone – she couldn't remember which. This knowledge seemed to reduce the experience to something less than romantic and romance, she thought, was important. Sitting on the edge of her bed she lifted her knee to her chin. She shook a bottle of nail varnish and began to paint her toe nails. A blood blister had developed on the end of her big toe. 'I know how I got this', she said to herself. She had been pedalling along next to Louisa earlier that day when her young companion had noticed a fresco painted on the side of a barn. This unusual sight made her wobble and she would have fallen off her bike had Cynthia not grabbed her handle bars and brought them to a halt. The blood blister must have been acquired at some point in this event. Louisa had left her bike in the middle of the road and walked back to the fresco to inspect it. Cynthia could see the rest of the party disappearing up the road and told Louisa to hurry up before they lost contact with them. Louisa seemed in no hurry and her absorbed attention was catching. Cynthia stood at Louisa's side as she traced her finger over the surface of the fresco, following the lines of an angel's wing and then the folds of the Virgin's dress. Cynthia recalled how Louisa had said 'Fra Somebody' and turned away and remounted her bike. Cynthia inspected her toe nails and then stroked the little varnish brush along each of her fingers. When she had finished she walked about her room shaking her hands and blowing on her nails alternately, and decided what to wear. Cynthia's idea of unpacking was to drape all of her clothes over chairs and tables and now she moved about the room picking up one garment after another until she had made her choice. Realising she was late for drinks before dinner she left her room in a flurry of chiffon and diamante.

"Dammit, Louisa, how on earth did you manage to do this?"

"Do what?"

"I don't know, but the pedals are shot and the chain keeps coming off. You've only been on the blasted thing for two days."

Daphne Bowler moved around her daughter's mountain bike tapping a universal spanner in her hand and then delivered her judgment.

"It's buggered. Signor Bignole, we will have to replace it."

"Scusi, signora?"

"Un altro. This is kaput."

Signor Bignole took in the bad news and wondered where 'un altro' could be sourced.   He knew that the lucrative bookings that flowed from the signora Inglese were dependent on his ability to solve any local problems that might arise. He wondered if his niece's ubiquitous knowledge of the young men in the village might be the answer.

"I ask around."

"Good but make it a sturdy one – Louisa, as you can see, has an unusual ability to wreck things."

"Scusi, signora?"

"Never mind. I'm off for a drink."

Louisa produced a sketch pad from her canvas bag and sitting on a low wall, crossed her long legs and pulled an HB pencil from behind her ear. She looked closely at a wild flower growing from the wall and began a drawing of its petals, stamen and its pale leaf veins. Beside the drawing she wrote in spidery letters ; 'neohtace-dod: peed atnegam/neerg elap'.

"Bello, bello."

"Thank you Mr B."

"Cosa c'e scritto qui?"

"The name of the plant and the colour of the flower and the colour of the leaf. I will paint it – dipingo – later."

"Ah, brava, brava."

"What news on the Rialto, mate?"

Duncan lowered a copy of The Times he had been delighted to find on sale in San Verino and beckoned Steve Durrant to join him.

"Beer?"

"Pope. Catholic."

"Nuff said."

Duncan waved in an ineffectual way to the aproned waiter and drained the remains of what was his second beer.

"Well?" said Steve.

"Trouble in the Caucasus. The big news seems to be that the Russians have cut the oil pipelines to the EU. Occupying Georgia was clearly just the first move. They're cosying up to China but we're out of favour. Shortages are predicted and panic buying is well under way. It looks as if we might have chosen the best mode of transport this summer."

"I would agree with you except my arse is telling me otherwise."

"You'll get used to it."

"You forgot to shave, I see," said Steve.

"Designer stubble, if you don't mind."

Duncan noticed that the rest of the party were converging on the Café Garibaldi and he rose to meet them. He could see Cynthia working her way from one shop to another and Mrs Bowler walking away from Louisa and Signor Bignole. He wondered where Lindsey had got to but then he saw him, a pink cashmere tied over his shoulders for all the world the Italian dandy.

"Is the missus all right about you being here?"

"I said she could come but it's a busy time at the moment. Big shifts in the market, recession looming and so on. Anyway, she was fine about me being away. Doesn't seem to mind. Encourages me, really. Gets me out of my domesticity."

"Right."

Duncan tapped the side of his beer glass and coughed.

"Time to think."

"Right."

"Gather ideas for sketches."

"And?"

Duncan tried to frame a sentence that would sum up what he was feeling but failed. Steve changed the subject.

"Good trips these. This year's a cracker, a bit out of the ordinary."

"Yes, makes a change from canoeing down the Wye," Duncan said relieved to be on firm ground again.

"Drafty guest houses."

"Leathery fried eggs."

"Packed lunches."

"'I walked the wall'. I've still got the tee shirt. Remember that one?" said Duncan.

"Northumbria, we stayed at Once Brewed."

"Twice Brewed."

"Are you sure?"

"No," Duncan laughed and went on, "It's been great not doing all the organizing. I left it all to Mrs Bowler. She was so relieved we'd agreed to take on Louisa. Two Wheels Good have done everything."

"I was worried we'd 'ave to put up with the boy friend," said Steve.

"Yes. I don't think her motives were entirely unselfish. The prospect of an unlimited supply of Italian waiters may have played its part in the plan."

Like a galley in full sail, Daphne Bowler appeared before them, her orange linen dress filling in the afternoon air. Duncan rose to his feet.

"Mrs Bowler."

"Andrew, do stop calling me by my surname. Daphne, please."

She surged past them and disappeared into the bar.

"Daft woman," said Steve.

"Yes. I quite like it really. Reminds me of being back at school. The past.

Another country. All that."

"Only posh gits would say that sort of thing. You'll be telling me next that you miss the sound thrashings that Flashman used to give you."

"It's odd really. I wonder what she thinks when she hears everyone else calling me Duncan?"

A battered construction lorry stopped on the other side of the piazza. Men with long handled spades began to dig up a length of cobbles. The door of the driver's cabin opened and Lucia and the driver jumped down and stood looking at the work in progress. Another man appeared with a long length of plastic piping and put it down next to the dusty trench that was emerging as the diggers piled the up-rooted cobbles and swung the heart shaped spades to deposit dusty earth into the back of the lorry. Lucia's companion was given a spade and he joined the others leaving Lucia on her own. A small crowd gathered to give the workers the benefit of their opinion about the best way to proceed; heads bowed as they peered at the gash in the ground. Lucia moved her weight from one leg to another, impatient at losing her companion to this communal interlude. Her separation from the herd was not lost on the predatory Lindsey who had been circling the piazza for some time reluctant to join his colleagues. Adjusting his cashmere he moved in on his prey. Standing next to Lucia he pretended to be just another bystander but then produced his cigarettes and the banal moves of the easy pick up were played out. Lucia, either from boredom or the realization that the Englishman would give her something the village boys would not be able to offer, responded with an oblique smile and an acceptance of the proffered gift.

Steve and Duncan watched as Pandora emerged through the plate glass doors of the Al Sole Hotel. She made her way hesitantly down the cobbled slope to the café, glancing to the left and right.

"What's she looking for?"

"Poor Pandora, not used to all this."

"She looks a bit unsteady on her pins. The Bird Woman's not on the neck oil is she?" said Steve.

"No. I think it's the heels. And don't call her the Bird Woman – it's unkind."

"Oh, beg pardon, I'm sure."

A voice behind them said:

"Hello boys, who are you eyeing up?"

"Cynthia, there you are. A little shopping?"

"Half the fun is getting these delicious bags."

Cynthia produced an assortment of pastel coloured scarves from an acid yellow carrier bag with the name UPIM on the side. Duncan nodded his approval and thought of Claire. He never shopped with his wife but was always shown the spoils of one of her infrequent visits to town. Claire would sit him in a chair and appear with different outfits, the rectangular 'designer' labels still attached. He would nod and say that each one was nice, or suited her well, or he liked the collar, or the colour. In all of this there was a sense that these ordinary moments were part of the binding that had kept them together for the best part of their adult lives. His thoughts were interrupted by Pandora who had finally negotiated her way to the gathering party.

"Oh, Duncan, this is simply lovely. I can't believe we're really here. You haven't seen a letter box have you?"

Pandora held up her postcard, her aquiline face looking pale and out of place. Sticking her other hand into the pocket of her beige cardigan, she pulled it around her thin body, the folds of her summer dress hanging loosely about her legs.

Daphne Bowler returned to the table, five bottles of Peroni hanging from her fingers. Steve pulled each one off her fingers with a little popping sound.

"I've ordered you a Martini, Pandora."

The piazza was suddenly alive with cyclists; the sleek, flattened tubing of a dozen racing machines powered by muscular riders, their epidermis of lycra vibrant with swirls of colour that matched the paint work of their bikes. As they leaned to take the bend there seemed no distinction between man and machine, the helmeted riders focusing through streamlined Ray Bans, their heads encased in polished, metalised tear drops.

"Bloody hell, d'you think they stopped for a breather at the top of the hill before making their grand entrance?"

"Probably not. Well cheers everyone, well met by..."

"Not quite moonlight, Duncan, but we get the point."

They were all together now: Lindsey, buoyed up by his encounter with the town beauty, positioned himself with his back to the wall so he could let his eyes linger on any passing young woman and so that they could see him; Pandora next to Duncan with her hands closed around her Martini as if it were a mug of cocoa; Steve his expansive rugby player's chest displaying a tee shirt that announced 'Jesus is Coming' and underneath in smaller letters 'Look Busy'; Mrs Bowler shouting across the square to Louisa telling her to join them and Louisa appearing not to hear.

"A toast. To Mrs Bowler, Daphne for making all this possible. It certainly beats Mrs Morgan's Glendower Guest House."

General agreement mingled with the chink of glass on glass.

"Now then, a little planning before dinner."

Daphne Bowler unfolded a map of the area and jabbed a finger at the city that lay a short distance from San Verino.

Parentals

Greeting from Bing Bong – well almost. Bing Baratat. Big island full of Real Gappers doing their bit for the developing (ie dirt poor) countries. Depressing meeting with a Jehovah Witness trying to convert the locals – not muslims – an older religion on the islands not sure what anyway he's not making much progress and said – hear this – the problem is they're happy with what they've got. Amazing. How did you know about the bucket? It's all right, I resisted it despite accusations of being a wimp. Have e mailed Sarah, no reply so far. Perhaps we're all in the dog house – nobody understands me etc She probably thinks I'm a pain in the arse – oooh 3 A Grades etc. Good luck, I turned out OK so you must be doing something right.

Simon Yoot

Glad to hear you're still selecting your destinations on the basis of their silly names. I remember we had a student from Vietnam once at De- Louche. His name was Phuck. I had to take him aside and have a word. I offered him some English names and he chose Simon– there was a thing. Am now in Italy with the college lot. Glorious weather, food to die for (and probably will if pasta intake continues at current rate). Your mother left to keep home fires burning which might entail putting the home fire out if your sibling decides to up the anti and go in for a bit of arson just to make her position on family life absolutely clear. Hey ho. Steve sends regards and Cynthia wants you to bring back some sarongs for her.

Love Dad

CHAPTER 13

UTTER HOPPE INSERTED A jemmy behind a wall bracket prising it away from the plaster. He held the bracket in his hands admiring the curved metal and the way it had been twisted to give it an air of art deco. Slipping the jemmy into his donkey jacket, he moved along the wall until he reached a group of people looking at a gilt framed painting which he guessed was seventeenth century Dutch, certainly not Vermeer but one of that school. A middle aged man was facing the group and pointing to the picture.
"The effect of space in a painting is primarily the creation of the illusion of three dimensions on a flat surface."

Utter produced a craft scalpel from his pocket and sliced through the tassle end of a rope that separated the paintings from the gallery viewers.

"Artists use various techniques to help them achieve this, a key one being the geometrical system known as linear or single view point perspective."

Standing close to the backs of the viewers he looked down at the electric colours of the tassle and moved on. He was having difficulty holding the Fire Exit sign that he had concealed inside his

jacket but steadied it on top of his trouser belt. A slim pedestal
with the words Way Out caught his eye. He took off his glasses
and rubbed them on white double cuffs that trumpeted, unbut-
toned from the sleeves of his jacket. Utter's glasses had thick black
frames around rectangular lenses. In keeping with his carefully
backswept hair he wore drainpipe trousers that tapered to a pair
of black leather boots, the points of which were capped with a
flash of steel. He considered how he might get the Way Out sign
out of the building but moved on when he saw that he was being watched by an attendant. Striding past a Bernini sculpture
made from white marble, he entered a side room. The words "I
Am Not Yet Something – See Me" had been pinned, in separate
letters, to the wall. On the floor was a fridge with its door open,
an assortment of domestic objects arranged so that they appeared
to be flowing from it. A tall, blonde woman with an Arab head-
dress wrapped around her throat and baggy Aladdin trousers was
speaking to a man who nodded and stared at the floor.

"It's in the moment, you see, that's what I am trying to capture.
Before any ideas are attached to it. While it's still free. Culturally
unhooked."

"Yes, yes, I see. But isn't it already too late if your work is here?"

Utter recognized a fellow spirit in the female artist but he had
work to do and scoped the room for any objects that might be
useful.

"The fridge is a symbol, we need to see our everyday lives as end-
lessly full of possibilities, to release them from …"

The woman's voice began to take on an elegiac tone and the man
stepped closer to the jumble of items on the floor. Utter took
advantage of their absorbed attention, finished his work and left
the room. When the woman had declaimed her manifesto, the
man pointed to the wall and said:

"Yes, I see, but perhaps you could explain that."

The message on the wall now read "I Am Not Yet Something – ee – e".

Utter stepped into the street and looked up at the Gothic façade of the gallery. A large bed sheet with the words "This is a prison – Utter Hoppe tells you this" was being hauled in by two attendants. Utter looked at his watch – his work had been up for one hour and seven minutes.

CHAPTER 14

DUNCAN TURNED THE NEWSSTAND until the headline of the Washington Post was facing him.

'Trade Dispute Escalates : Belarus Government backs Russia.'

"Come on Duncan. Getting away from the news is part of the holiday."

Duncan and Cynthia had decided to bike the short distance from San Verino to the city while the others had taken the train. Cynthia took Duncan by the arm and led him back to his bike. He folded his trouser bottoms and tucked them into his socks. Cynthia hitched her skirt trapping it as she sat down. They waited by the kerb for the traffic from the nearby lights to flow past them and then pushed into the road. They passed shops and apartment blocks along tree lined avenues and saw ahead of them the bulk of a medieval city wall. Two bailey towers were separated by an arched entrance in front of which was a roundabout. A lorry loaded with vegetables moved slowly around the roundabout and bumped over the cobbled surface beneath the city wall. A jumble of red tiled roofs and television aerials massed behind the ancient wall and above all of them the peaks and slopes of a mountain range. Duncan and Cynthia wove around a long queue of traffic that led away from a petrol station. Some of the drivers were standing by their cars or walked up the line and talked to other drivers, gesticulating to the head of the queue. Car horns were blown followed by irritated cries. As Duncan reached the road outside the forecourt he saw a man bending over five jerry cans methodically filling each in turn. Reaching the city wall the two cyclists passed under the archway and stared up at a bas relief coat of arms topped by a cardinal's hat. It became difficult to ride over the cobbled street and so they dismounted weaving through the late morning shoppers. Duncan stopped outside a shop window that advertised 'cambio' and cheap rate telephone calls to cities across the world. In the middle of the window was a large hand written poster that announced "Internet – 1 Euro – 5 Minutes".

"You go on, Cynthia. I'll just catch up with the family."

Duncan tapped in his email address and waited. There were one or two other users in the little café which was divided up into makeshift cubicles painted lime green. A bored looking girl sat on a stool by the cash till and filed her nails. Moments of emotion flickered across the faces of the customers as they gazed at their screens and an occasional mutter escaped from their lips as they responded to their electronic interlocutors. There was something of the madhouse about all of this, as if internal worlds were being glimpsed and the personal made audible. He had two emails – one from Claire and one from Simon. He opened Claire's first anticipating his daughter's latest delinquent episode and preferring to get it out of the way.

Dearest Dunc

Joy, Sarah has a new boyfriend. He's called Fist. He never speaks and as far as I can see possesses only one t shirt (Al Pacino with machine gun) and trousers that an anorexic would find difficulty getting into. Your daughter and the Fist have reduced human experience to a wordless, inert domain. They hold court in the sitting room. I am allowed to clean around them as long as I don't interfere with daytime TV too much. Work is quite exciting if a little scary – credit crunches, rising price of oil, etc. Really puts us all on our mettle. Nothing to worry lotus eaters like yourself. Missing you lots.

Love Claire xxx

Duncan sighed the weary sigh of the long distance parent. Opening the email from Simon he saw only a scramble of letters and hieroglyphs. He paid his 1 Euro, disappointed that he had been unable to open his son's email.

CHAPTER 15

The 'Leonardo da Vinci: the mind of a scientist' exhibition was held in a Palladian mansion in a back street of the city. Massive pillars circled the reception area and the paying public thronged around the ticket office. Louisa moved awkwardly through the crowd looking for her companions, the sounds of a dozen languages swirling and eddying around her. She had lost touch with the others and was on her own. Fortunately the exhibition was advertised on banner posters all over the city and by a process of stopping people and pointing to the poster, Louisa had edged her way to the right place without the mournful and endless traipsing that normally accompanied being lost. Feeling pleased with herself for finding her own way but anger at being abandoned, Louisa moved towards the box office and tried to remember the word for ticket – Biletto, bigetto, something with o on the end of it.

"One ticket, please. Student."

Louisa rummaged in her bag and produced a dog eared card.

"Out of date," the ticket attendant tapped her student card and said:

"Next."

The world returned to being a difficult place where this sort of thing happened all the time. Louisa paid the full price and wandered away into the crowd. She dropped her card into a bin. She could usually shrug off these moments of wretched inadequacy but now her whole history pressed upon her like a rising tide of bile that threatened to overcome her. Her fragile 'amour propre' quivered against the hounds of persecution that bayed 'useless, useless' as she descended into darkness. Her breath came in short bursts, sweat beading across her forehead. It had always been like this, she thought. She remembered sitting in a consulting room with her mother and a man in a suit explaining in a cheerful voice that 'Louisa's brain is just wired differently' as if this were a good thing, as if not knowing if Tuesday came before or after Wednesday (or not knowing anything) were OK.

When she was ten her mother had moved house to be near a school with a good special needs department. Daphne Bowler was not sure what 'good' meant in this context but thought it was worth a shot. Louisa had spent her days in a portacabin in an atmosphere of suppressed violence with an assortment of delinquents and the chronically disaffected. The unit was presided over by Mrs Prince who had told Louisa that dyslexia was a gift, a concept that, like every other concept, Louisa had found hard to grasp. At break times while the other students fanned out across the campus to find the criminal groups from whom they had been temporarily disconnected, Louisa stayed behind. Retrieving pieces of paper from the recycling box she sat by the window and opened her pencil case. She had been given her Pocahontas pencil case when she started primary school – its shiny surface battered and worn from use. Taking 'Wild Animals' down from a shelf she copied one or other of the pictures until the bell went and the other inmates scuffled back into the room.

"Lu, how did you get here?"

Daphne stood over her daughter and they went through a well rehearsed litany of recrimination and blame. Louisa ran her long fingers over her face poking her forefinger into one nostril and then the other before moving on to her ears.

"Do stop doing that. We've agreed to meet back here in one hour. One hour. If you're not here ..."

"...we'll go without you. I know," Louisa said flatly.

Squeezing past a group of Chinese tourists Louisa entered a large white- washed room entitled 'The Moon and the Sky', in the middle of which was a glass case containing an astrolabe and on the walls pages from da Vinci's notebooks. One of the pages showed a shaded orb with a white finger nail edge on one side. Louisa read the label beside it:

"Codex Leicester, Sheet 2A folio 2r

Leonardo is credited with the first correct explanation of why the crescent moon in twilight sky shows a gentle glow across its unilluminated parts ......"

On the walls next to this exhibit was a drawing showing sunlight reflecting from earth and illuminating the unlit portion of a crescent moon. The drawing imitated the style and arrangement of the da Vinci pages to suggest that the genius himself had popped in to make things clearer to a benighted public. Louisa moved to the next exhibit. It showed a page of handwritten script on paper that was so thin as to be translucent. Long, thick stems of p's and b's and l's punctuated lines of spidery lettering and were lost among other letters visible from the other side of the page. Louisa wasn't expecting to be able to read this ancient manuscript but she couldn't make out any words, even Italian ones. Then it came to her. This was a page of backwards writing. This was how she wrote! She looked at the writing again but this time read from right to left. It still didn't seem to make the right sounds. Opening her handbag she produced a little make up mirror and held it up to the exhibit – 'formato maggiore quanto.'

"You've worked it out. He was a lefty, he didn't want to get his sleeve inky."

Louisa turned to see the spiky figure of Utter Hoppe pushing his spectacles onto the bridge of his nose and smiling down at her. She wanted to tell this stranger that she wrote like da Vinci – well almost – but her habit of concealment stopped her.

"Cool."

"Utter Hoppe. Artist. And you are?"

"Louisa Bowler," Louisa wanted to say that she, too, was an artist but didn't think that a few sketches and two pencils qualified her.

"Enjoy."

And he moved away. Louisa noticed Utter seemed to be looking for something and didn't look at any of the exhibits.

'Fossils and the Flood' came next. Louisa's discovery of kinship to Leonardo sharpened her interest in the great man. She read that Leonardo had seen that the biblical flood was an inadequate explanation of why fossils were found at the top of mountains. Standing back to take in Da Vinci's depiction of time and motion over millennia, Louisa saw Utter sitting with his head between his knees on a studded ottoman in the middle of the room. At first he looked as if he was ill but his hand moved across the floor between his legs and gathered she knew not what. She turned back to a minute sketch of a shell surrounded by the now familiar scrawl. Turning away, she noticed that Utter was back on his feet and was standing in a corner of the room – his body looked as if he might be about to urinate, his arms appearing to make the same movement men did in the street near her home in North London when they were undoing their flies preparatory to relieving themselves against a wall. Unwilling to be present when he was hauled off by the attendants Louisa made her exit.

The next room was very crowded and simply had the word 'Flight' to tell the visitor what it contained. This was the centrepiece of the exhibition and Da Vinci's winged human figure magnified a hundred times appeared on the walls along with other images of his work. In the middle of the room was a plinth on top of which was a scale model of da Vinci's helicopter. Around the plinth was a cordon keeping the visitors two metres away from the exhibit. Louisa decided to keep this to the last and began to move around the perimeter of the room. Utter appeared next to her.

"Better?"

"What?"

"What were you doing in there?"

"Collecting."

Utter bent down and picked up a discarded exhibition ticket. Leonardo's self portrait was torn in the middle, the two sides folded together so that the bearded face appeared to have one elongated eye and no nose.

"Da Vinci the Cyclops," Utter said and showed Louisa.

"Very funny. What have you got in your jacket?"

Utter undid one of his buttons revealing the letter DA.

"It says Da Vinci Toilets."

"Right."

"I have enough now."

"Enough for what?" she asked.

"Come, let us look at the flying machine."

Louisa and Utter stood before the little model, its delicate under-cone encasing a sliver of metal twisted into a spring above which the flattened helter skelter of the screw, with its paper membrane creased with age, sat slightly lopsided on the cone. Next to the exhibit were scraps of paper made to look as if they were from Da Vinci's note book. Each one showing a part of the helicopter and inscribed with mirror writing.

"I have to go now. Do you want to come with me?"

"OK."

Utter and Louisa stood with their backs to the Palladian museum.

"Which way shall we go?" Louisa said.

"First close your eyes and put out your hand."

"Ooh, surprises."

Louisa closed her eyes and held out her hand.

"You can open now," Utter said.

Louisa looked down at a scrap of paper curling in her palm. She saw mirror writing and a drawing of the helter skelter screw.

"Utter! How did you get this? You must put it back."

"It's only a mocked up label – they can make another one. I thought you'd like it – after all you both write the same way. What does it say?"

" I can't tell. Thank you. It's a nice present."

As they walked away from the museum Utter told Louisa to look back.

A long streamer fell from one of the entrance pillars. It read:

Dada

Les

Vinci

-

Utter Hoppe

"Thirty eight minutes and still there. Not bad," Utter was pleased.

"Cool."

CHAPTER 16

DUNCAN STOOD BY A wall covered in posters advertising musical performances and looked at Utter's streamer and wondered how it had got there and what it meant. Was this an installation and an official part of the exhibition and, if it was, what was he and the rest of the paying public to make of it? He read the message again and wondered if the name was an elaborate anagram. He wrote out the letters on the back of his exhibition catalogue: TOPER HOTE, RUTTE HOP. What was this 'les'? Was there more than one Hoppe? THE POPE RULES. Perhaps that was it, Had the Pontiff looked around the Vatican and chosen two of his most athletic cardinals to take the faith to the people. Had he succumbed to the modern age and targeted art lovers and intellectuals as the most lapsed members of his flock who needed to be spoken to in their own language? Was this Opus Dei going Pop? He imagined the muscular cardinals putting on their purple track suits and setting off for the museum, the banner rolled under their arms. That, at least, would give the banner a kind of credence. However, if there was no Catholic branch of the postmodern movement, and on reflection Duncan thought this unlikely, then what was this all about? If this was modernism it seemed to Duncan to have slipped from the ironic to the merely jokey. He could feel himself being drawn into disapproval, to an earnest rejection of 'this sort of thing' and a retreat into a mindset that ruled certain things in and certain things out, this painted bedsheet belonging firmly to the ruled out group. Then he got it. The banner was subversive, undermining the certainty of received ideas that depended on things that were OK and things that were not OK. Duncan moved from foot to foot and turned coins over in his pockets and muttered 'bloody hell'. In an attempt at bringing things back to a stable state he attacked the jokeyness as immature, as the privilege of the young who had nothing to lose but who, in their denigration of what had come before, descended into triviality and spent their time on pranks like the one he was now looking at. But if he was not joining in, if he was saying no to all this did that not make him an old fogey defending the declared 'canon' and the airless vaults of tradition and inheritance. This didn't feel right either. He looked back at the banner that was moving in smooth ripples with the gentle Italian air that seemed to say: 'It's alright. Relax. Let go a little.' Duncan felt the temptations of dissolution. Was the banner saying that everything was art? Yes, he'd heard that, he knew that was what the jokeyness was about. He felt trapped by age. He could not join in with the joke, for in doing so there would be a double suspicion that he was performing the intellectual equivalent of wearing cut off jeans; that he was trying to hang on to a youth that had gone and that his own tribe would reject this relativism, this loosening of standards. He consoled himself with the thought that none of it mattered really but in the same moment he knew that there was something in this that he could not ignore.

Two small windows opened either side of the pillar where the banner hung. Duncan watched as a gallery attendant emerged from each window like two jacks-in-a-box. At the base of the column a small crowd was being ushered away by other attendants. They craned their necks upwards and shouted "Va bene" and the jacks-in-the-box began to cut the strings that attached the banner to the pillar. Holding the released banner for a moment and checking that all was clear they let go. The material clung to the pillar, picking out its sharp crests and then folded itself like a sail filling with wind. One of the attendants on the ground had fallen into conversation with someone in the crowd so that when the sheet reached the ground it lapped over him. There was a moment of struggle as he tried to release himself from the material before he emerged to the applause of the crowd. The sheet was folded carefully and taken in through the museum entrance. Duncan imagined that it might be taken to a damp cellar, hung upside down and interrogated by Old Masters who would extract a confession from this upstart for daring to question the verities of high art. The Duke of Urbino would be there along with Lippi's St Bernard and a Medici or two. They would have the last laugh as they tore the sheet to shreds, slowly, the screams of the banner unheard by the visitors on the floor above.

Deciding not to wait for the others, Duncan made his way to his bike. He would leave a note on Cynthia's saddle. This opportunity to be on his own was not to be missed and anyway he found it less stressful negotiating the traffic by himself. He leant the machine towards him so that he only had to lift his left leg a little off the vertical and settled himself on the seat. Claire had insisted that he take a helmet with him but, so far, he had not worn it. The spirit of adventure seemed to be dulled by wearing a helmet and the associations of wind rushing through sweptback hair were too powerful for Duncan to resist. Besides, there was something of the health and safety culture about cycle helmets that Duncan instinctively disliked. As he shifted into sixth gear and kept abreast of the slow moving traffic he also realized that his non compliance was about as close to a mid-life crisis as he was likely to get. Not wearing a helmet was a statement of independence and a retrieval of the past. Duncan thought about the swaying length of Utter's

white banner and he thought of a time, years ago, when he had
seen another building defaced by revolution. He had been hitch-
hiking on a roadside some sixty kilometres from Milan and was
picked up by someone of his own age returning to university.
When they arrived it was like entering a battle zone.   Broken
traffic bollards and lumps of masonry were strewn across the road
and groups of riot police leaned against barricades. There was an
air of relaxed hiatus, the police offering cigarettes to each other
and chatting to students on a picket line. The front of the main
building was covered in political slogans. Here and there whole
tins of red paint had been slung at the walls creating a Jackson
Pollock effect across windows and doors. Duncan's companion,
a mountainous figure with a beard worthy of Captain Haddock,
had taken Duncan by the arm and led him to a side door where
he had announced his arrival in the raucous tones of the Milanese.
The door was eased open and they were pulled into a huge room,
busy with the activities of revolt. Duncan's companion was
greeted with cries of delight, his soubriquet of 'Tiny' adding to
the atmosphere of humorous camaraderie. Duncan was taken to
a refectory table heaped with the detritus of a hurriedly prepared
meal. He was surrounded by young men, their fresh complexions
at odds with the revolutionary beards they had cultivated and a
chunk of bread with a mess of salami slices was placed in front
of him. A young woman with blazing auburn hair dressed in a
black tee shirt and trousers filled a plastic cup with red wine and
handed it to him. He had not eaten for two days and fell on his
food while the young Marxists, mistaking him for an American,
asked him about sit ins at Berkeley (perhaps he had been there?)
and railed against the iniquities of the fascist home guard who
had opened fire at Kent State. The young Duncan fielded these
questions as best he could, his interest in food overwhelming any
feelings of political injustice that, in reality, he never felt, hungry or not. He remembered spending the rest of the day with
them: copying aphorisms from Trotsky and Marx and tracing an
enormous hammer and sickle on a packing case that had been

flattened into a placard. Sometime after midnight sleeping bags were dragged onto stained mattresses and the exuberant chatter had ebbed and faded into sleep, Duncan contriving to lie next to the auburn haired beauty. He thought about Utter Hoppe and the young Marxists and time contracted so that they seemed to exist at the same time in the same place, the present belonging to the past and the past being present in the moment. He tried to remember the lines from Ecclesiastes, 'for everything there is a season' and something about 'a time to destroy and a time to build up'. He thought about that time in Milan with its mixture of intensity and passion and something else, some intangible lightness that was always dying and being reborn. Duncan had reached the outskirts of the city now, the anodyne facades of 'mobili' megastores and the names of international trade – Siemens, IBM, Sony – jutting from multicoloured prefabricated offices on either side of the road. The crowded city buildings gave way to suburban villas, their shaded gardens festooned by grapevines and eventually Duncan was pedalling between fields that rolled away from him in waves of patched light.

Darling D

It gets worse! I arrived home yesterday to find a big laundry bag in the hall. Sarah and Simon – yes, Simon!- (I found out his real name from Mrs Pike and refuse to call him Fist – horrible name) were in their usual horizontal position in the sitting room. I asked about the bag and Sarah told me that Simon had had a row with his Dad and that he had walked out and had nowhere else to go. From this I gathered that he was now staying with us! Simon just looked at me. The row had been about his lack of work, usual stuff – ironic or what! Anyway, he's no trouble and actually did a bit of washing up last night.

Love Claire xxx

CHAPTER 17

"I'm sure she'll be all right Daphne. She is eighteen after all. She'll've fallen in with some other young people and be having a great time."
"Always threatened to leave without her, never actually done it. But where is the girl."

Cynthia Digit put a hand on Daphne's arm and smiled reassuringly at her.

"Look, she probably thought it would be OK to go off since she knew we were going to be here for a couple of days. I did see her talking to some young people. An opportunity to get away from the oldies for a bit. You know."

Cynthia did not tell Louisa's mother that it had not been some young people, rather that it had been one young person, but he had looked harmless and when she had seen Utter and Louisa they had seemed to be having a nice time.

"Thing is, she's on another planet most of the time, doesn't know where she is. Might be …taken advantage of. I shouldn't have let you persuade me to leave her."

"Perhaps she needs to find her own way a little."

"What do you mean?"

"Just that really. Anyway, I'm sure she'll turn up soon."

The two women turned away from each other and leaned on a low wall that bordered one side of the San Verino piazza. Long shadows fell on the kitchen gardens that clung to the terraced hillside below the wall. A monorail track wound through orchards and patches of cultivated land. Cynthia and Daphne watched as a man in light blue overalls walked beside an electric engine pulling three little wagons laden with produce. The man stopped by an olive tree and laid a sheet beneath its gnarled branches. The engine went on through the olive grove and emerged into cooling sunlight as the man braced himself against the trunk of the tree and began a slow rhythm that shook the branches and covered the sheet with the fallen olives. Gathering the edge of the sheet he slung it over his shoulder. Catching up with the engine that was now struggling up an incline, he slowed his pace and man and machine moved on together.

"Clever. He must have done that a thousand times."

"Sorry, Cynthia, can't enjoy it not knowing where the young 'un is. What if she's had an accident – you saw what she did to her bike yesterday. Perhaps we should tell the police."

"Tell them what?"

Cynthia beckoned to Steve who was crossing the piazza.

"Oh, Steve. Tell Daphne here not to worry. Louisa's not back yet."

Steve said: "I spoke to her when we were leaving. She was with a young fella, seemed to be a nice lad. He looked like Elvis Costello

– not that you can hold that against him. Arty type. She seemed quite happy. You mustn't worry."

Normally, Daphne Bowler was not one to make a fuss. Indeed her brisk sense for business was founded on a distrust of intro-spection. Her inner world was populated by a pantheon of logical and clearly defined thoughts whose existence depended on exter-nal realities. Balance sheets and cost benefit analysis ruled every aspect of her life. The murky recesses of self doubt had been banished long ago and in their place she had erected temples to the entrepreneurial spirit and palaces of managerial strategy. As a young woman of no means 'One Minute Manager' had been her Bible and when Margaret Thatcher had declared that there was no such thing as society it had seemed to legitimize the power games that were the foundation of her business successes. One of her fondest memories as a child was the day she had first served customers in her parents' hardware store in Hastings. Standing on an upturned milk crate behind the counter she had played shop for real and asked a middleaged woman what she could get her. She remembered turning to a pyramid of Duraglit Silvo and carefully taking down the topmost tin. She held it for a moment in her hand and looked at the Japanese flag design carried out in white and silver rays. The patented product label at the centre of the rays declared that the contents were 'Long Lasting' and that the tin contained 'Silver Polish Wadding'. She had mouthed the word 'wadding' and had liked the feel of it on her lips. Turning to her customer she had placed the tin on the counter and as-sured her that 'good wadding this is' and told her the price. As the heavy pre-decimalization coins were counted into her small palm she became the centre of the spreading rays of white and sil-ver and the moment stretched and the power of this commercial epiphany was indelibly imprinted on her consciousness and from it flowed a self assurance that coincided with a changing world in which the rise of Roddick and Branson and Sugar confirmed Daphne Bowler's path in life. The brief interlude of which Louisa had been the inconvenient product had been the only episode to find Daphne Bowler on the back foot. She had fallen for Hans when they had met as fellow buyers at a fashion fair in Antwerp. He had bought her a drink in the bar of their hotel and chatted to her about which designer labels were likely to be the next 'big thing'. They gossiped about Versace and Yves and Daphne took in his confidence and his good looks. Hans was the archetypal German, courteous and correct and oozing controlled dominance. When they met again the following evening he had taken her to his room and made love to her with a tenderness that she was unused to. When the fair ended they stayed on for a week, most of which was spent in bed and at the end of which Daphne was pregnant. When he left her to return to Stuttgart he had promised to come to London the following month – she never saw him again. Daphne had been amazed at the breathtaking way he had managed to unpick all her defences so that she had let him in without conditions. She had been equally shocked by the clinical way in which he had left her, the months following her abandonment being a slow parabola of fading pain. This, too, had been a kind of epiphany, another moment of clarity and re-solve, the 'never again' resulting in relationships of convenience and control. During these brief affairs with men who served their purpose Louisa had been looked after by a series of childminders and, when Daphne began to earn good money, nannies. Daphne had decided early on that she was not cut out to be a mother and this had legitimized her neglect. It was only when it became clear that Louisa had what the educational world delicately called 'learning difficulties', and Daphne called 'thick', that she took an interest in her. The challenge of getting local authorities to lay on adequate provision suited her combative nature rather than any empathy for Louisa who had merely become the football be-tween her mother and the opposing side of ed psychs, SENCO's and the machinery behind a succession of statements of special educational needs. Daphne had read all the legislation, had con-sulted specialist lawyers and had gone into appeal meetings with chapter and verse and fought the good fight and had gone home to Louisa and been exasperated with her and given her food and shelter but little more. And now this Achilles heel, this hesitation of care in the face of her disappearance that had no satisfactory explanation.

"I've asked Signore Bignole to go down to the station and wait for the next few trains. He's taken the van so she doesn't have to bike back up the road," Steve said.

"Thank you."

"Come on, grub up. They're serving in the dining room."

Respected Elders

Sorry about long gap haha but Sonny and I have been to another beach party that went on for two weeks. Usual heady mix of sex, drugs and rock and roll (sic). Didn't think you'd want to hear about that so here's something to amuse you. On day ten and beginning to feel the strain of unbridled hedonism (sick) fell into company with a lad from Birmingham. He'd arranged with a friend who was staying in Jakarta to send e mails to his parents every two days telling them about interesting sites he had visited as a cover for a little excursion to the beach party. Anyway after a bit his parents had smelt a rat and registered the Brummie as a missing person with the FO. Our man in Jak. was dispatched to find him and , knowing a thing or two about we rebellious yoot, made straight for the party. So here we were taking our ease under a coconut tree when a motor launch appears and a man dressed in a white suit – I kid you not - jumps ashore and makes a bee line for us. He tells our new chum that his mother would like to hear from him. Severe loss of beach cred. and off he goes to brood on the injustices of life etc. Sonny and I howling.

Love, Simon

Simon

Ah! Man is born free but everywhere is tied to the apron strings. Mothers, eh? The power to move mountain when required. News from the home front: Mother has told you about the boyfriend – a member of the emu (emo? emi?) community and thus able to maintain a monastic silence even in the face of determined middle class politeness. He has clearly read his Leary and decided that noone over thirty is to be trusted and this has confirmed Sarah's general approach to the bulk of humanity. Spot of bother here – after brief visit to a museum one of the Two Wheels Good party has jumped ship. She's only eighteen so there's a bit of concern for her well being. Local police involved and we've suspended holiday until the wretched girl turns up. Got to go. Search Party meeting being called.

Love Dad

CHAPTER 18

PANDORA TOOK A WET wipe from her travelling make up case and drew it across her forehead and cheeks. She craned her neck to look at the TV suspended from a metal arm high up on her bedroom wall. She had spent some time reading the laminated card which contained obscure instructions about the operation of the pay channels that included, in bold type, the offer of 'channali adulte' before abandoning it and randomly flicking through the channels, eventually settling on the CNN news. A blonde woman looked squarely into the camera and announced the news headlines. She was indistinguishable from female newsreaders the world over. Luxurious hair fell on the shoulders of a Dior suit from which rose an elegant neck that betrayed an age inconsistent with her groomed and youthful good looks. Wide, baby eyes were combined with an earnest expression. The firm, thin lips of the experienced journalist announcing news from Darfur and Gaza and Chechnya. Pandora thought that here was a woman who knew what she was about and who had, no doubt done a tour of duty in these places. Pandora began to read the tickertape strip at the bottom of the screen – the world seemed to be carrying on as normal with its litany of bloodletting and crises. The Russian oil embargo ran seamlessly into further evidence of the impending tipping point in climate change and the continuation of US 'rendition' activities. Pandora experienced her usual feeling of mild depression at all of this, a dull ache that arose from the thought that there seemed very little hope for humanity when the resources of nations seemed to be focused on mutual destruction. The screen showed a picture that Pandora recognized but was only able to place it when she realized she was looking at the art gallery they had visited that day. In the background and only partly in shot, she could see a little group looking up at a white sheet as it slithered down the face of the building. In the foreground a news reporter stood with his face partly obscured by a large honeycomb microphone.

"Months of speculation have now been ended by the announcement that the Da Vinci helicopter model is, in fact, the real thing. The art world has long been aware that this might be the case and carbon testing has now confirmed that the little model in the exhibition behind me was made by Da Vinci himself in 1499. Curators at the museum are expecting even greater visitor numbers and new security measures have been put in place. In a further development, Curators announced that a page …"

Pandora pressed a red button on the remote and the screen went black. She reached up to put the stand-by light off, ran a brush through her hair and left the room. She wanted to be the first to tell everybody about the exhibit they had all admired that day and hoped that no one else had beaten her to it.

A squall of wind carried leaves through the air and rain swept across San Verino making her ancient cobbles and flagstones glisten black. The waiter at the Café Garibaldi appeared with a long winding handle under his arm, like a medieval knight with a jousting pike, and began to retract the sun awning. A lime coloured door next to the café opened and the urbane figure of Lindsey appeared. As he stepped away from the door he looked up at an open window where the shadowy outline of Signore Bignole's niece was arranging her hair and buttoning her white blouse in readiness for another day at the Al Sole. Duncan stood at the window of the breakfast room and watched as people made their way from shop to shop, provisioning for the day. He thought about his Saturday morning visits to Waitrose with Claire and wondered at the simplicity of these people's lives. There seemed none of the frenzied movement of supermarket shopping where trolleys were heaped from homogenous rows of products giving an illusion of choice. He noticed that these people were able to fit all their needs into one or two bags, shopping as they were, one day at a time. He imagined the fresh foods being unpacked in apartment kitchens amid the chatter of family gossip, children being dispatched to fetch herbs and steady, accustomed hands gripping stainless steel knives to pare and gut and slice vegetables and fish and meats.

"Oh, Duncan, there you are. Have you seen the news?"

"No, Pandora, Cynthia told me I wasn't to. I've been watching the locals. They seem to have all the time in the world – even on a rainy day."

"Ah, the rose tinted specs. of the tourist."

"Maybe. Anyway, what news?"

"The Da Vinci flying machine."

"What about it?" Duncan said.

"It's real. I mean it's not just any old model. Da Vinci made it himself. In 1499. Much older than they thought. It's been authenticated as Da Vinci's.

Isn't it exciting?"

Pandora looked around and realized that they were alone. She had a sudden recollection of looking up at Duncan as he powered their punt up the Cherwell.

"Shall we have a little breakfast. Do join me."

Pandora blushed as an association of breakfast and a night of passion overwhelmed her. They turned to a long table laid out for breakfast. A pile of white plates and rows of silver cutlery were arranged at one end of the table and along its length glass bowls containing various fruits swimming in orange and grapefruit juice. Pandora moved past these to three dishes heaped with unfamiliar pastries beside which were little packets of butter and vacuum sealed conserves. Duncan reached to the back of the table where a row of silver cylinders promised a less European choice. Sliding the curved metal opening on its embossed hubs, Duncan revealed a mess of scrambled eggs. He scooped a small amount onto his plate and opened another. This time button mushrooms crowded one end of the cylinder and at the other end crisp slices of bacon curled and interwoven so that Duncan had to hack a square section free before he could add this to his plate.

"Never any toast."

Pandora gripped a long roll and offered it to him.

"This will have to do instead."

In taking the bread their fingers touched briefly. Pandora looked directly at Duncan and her cheeks blushed again.

"Coffee?"

Pandora Fulbright suddenly felt the futility of her feelings but instead of self recrimination, she attacked Duncan. This man was like all the other men she had considered in the past – very polite, very respectable and completely incapable of the levels of passion and intimacy that she felt were essential if a relationship were to have any meaning at all. She looked at the bald patch beginning to appear at the back of his head and his hunched shoulders as he poured the coffee and condemned him for not being remotely like Rochester – there had been that moment of manly power on the river but he clearly did not have the sensibility to play opposite her Jane Eyre. Where were these men whose primitive force was irresistible, the Darcys and the Heathcliffs? Perhaps they only existed in books. She looked down at her ringless and bony hands and gave in to the realities that governed her spinster existence. She had been unkind to Duncan and was relieved when the breakfast room doors opened and the rest of the group arrived.

"Not in her room. I'm off to report this. The police probably won't do a thing but I can't stand just sitting about. At least they could check hospitals and what not," Daphne said despondently.

Steve Durrant poured coffee for everyone and brought a large plate of pastries to the table.

"What about hiring a car, doing a bit of investigating ourselves?"

"Tried that. None to be had and anyway the Russians have made it impossible to get any petrol – I don't fancy running out in the middle of nowhere."

"Shouldn't we just wait here?" said Pandora.

Duncan considered this for a moment but looked at Daphne's anxious face and realized that action was called for.

"No. We've got the bikes. We'll find her ourselves."

CHAPTER 19

DAPHNE BOWLER SAT IN the reception area of the District 2 police station and wondered how long she was going to be kept waiting. The grey, distempered walls were bare except for a laminated poster listing obscure regulations and by-laws. She had arrived sometime earlier armed with the phrase 'I wish to report a missing person' in Italian and hoping the dramatic nature of this statement would trigger a flurry of activity. Instead, the two young police officers ignored her, sipping Starbucks coffee from takeaway cups and scanning the local newspaper. Finding what they were looking for they let out groans of disappointment. Daphne understood this 'mis en theatre' when both men reached into their trouser pockets and produced lottery tickets which they tore up, dropping the scraps of paper into a wire mesh wastepaper bin. Turning their attention to the foreign woman they asked her what she wanted. Daphne had been momentarily distracted from the sick feeling in her stomach by their dark good looks, their well-cut uniform jackets accentuating their slim figures. The scarlet stripes on their trousers disappearing into polished leather boots had been particularly arousing. Gathering herself she repeated her statement with renewed force.

"I wish to report a missing person."

Without replying, one of the officers moved towards a grey stacker unit and pulled open one of the drawers, its metallic screech underlining the drabness of the place.

"Fill in."

The officers turned their backs and fell to routine filing and typing and exchanged occasional remarks. Had she not been so worried Daphne would have found this atmosphere of normality soothing; as it was, she thought that it was just another part of the theatre designed to heighten her anxiety. Daphne began to decipher the form as well as she could, the banal questions keeping her racing imagination at bay. Realising that this was merely a bureaucratic exercise designed to delay the need for the officers to do anything, she slapped the pen onto the desk and tried to think of the Italian for 'I want to see a senior officer'.

"Look here, this isn't good enough. I need to speak to someone in English. Inglese."

The telephone rang.

"Pronto. Si. Si."

A mumbled conversation followed in which the officer occasionally looked at Daphne. Replacing the receiver he turned to his colleague.

"Avante."

Daphne watched as they fitted dark blue pudding bowl helmets to their sleek heads and left the room. There was a moment of complete silence and another door opened. A bulky figure dressed in a gaberdine coat came towards her. He put out a hand and bowed.

"Inspector Giuseppe Grippe, signora. Please. Sit."

Daphne detected something other than Italian in his English accent but could not place it.

"Thank you inspector. I thought I was going to be here all day."

"It is a busy time for us. The summer visitors, the Da Vinci exhibition and this news of authenticity, the petrol shortage. It all makes work for us. How can I help you?"

Inspector Grippe looked at Daphne through bloodshot eyes. He had spent most of the night sitting in his unmarked car outside an apartment block watching the movements of petty thieves and local drug dealers. The few arrests would help his crime figures but little else was achieved, he knew he would be arresting the same people in a few months time.

"It's my daughter. She's gone missing."

Daphne squeezed folds of skin at her neck so that these words came out in a strangled whisper.

"And when was this? When did you last see her?"

"Yesterday. We were at the exhibition but she didn't meet up with us as planned."

"As planned?"

"Yes. You see, I was trying to be, to let her have her head a bit."

"Have her head?"

"Give her a bit of freedom."

"What is her name?"

"Louisa. Anyway, she didn't turn up and still wasn't back this morning."

Daphne paused and said "I'm sick with worry" and hung her head. Inspector Grippe did not speak for a moment.

" Signora Bowler, your daughter will be back with you very soon, I guarantee."

"How do you know?"

"They always turn up once they have had their little adventure."

"This may be routine to you but it's my daughter you're talking about. And what do you mean by 'little adventure'?"

Inspector Grippe regretted that his tiredness had made him sound indifferent but the pattern was very familiar. This Louisa, he thought, has done the sights and galleries and then, like all the others, looks for a little more excitement. Enter Fabio or Fiorgio or Angelo. He's heard that these visitors are not like the girls he knows, they are not surrounded by an impregnable wall of mothers and Inspector Grippe knew the boy would rely on the reputation of the hot Italian lover to make him desirable to these pale, beautiful girls. He discovers that many of them are not easily seduced but does not dwell on the failure of his sugary compliments or his offers to give them a ride on his Lambretta. This is because, the Inspector thought wearily, for every ten that are able to resist there will be one who is not and who will go with him up unlit alleys after an evening of Peronis and laughter and let him do things to her that Carla and Micol and Adriana would never allow.

"Signora Bowler, every summer we have young people – boys and girls – who 'go missing' and their parents sit where you are sitting and tell me they are worried. And their son or their daughter always turns up, after a day or two days. You must not worry."

"But what if she has had an accident?"

"The form you have filled in will be all we need. The hospitals will be contacted and the police stations in the other city districts. I have your hotel telephone number and we will be in touch when we hear anything."

"If you hear anything."

"Signora, trust me. Your daughter is safe and will come back to you soon. Now, it has been a long night. I must go home."

CHAPTER 20

THE LITTLE COPSE OF walnut trees beneath the town wall of San
Verino provided Cynthia Digit with shade from the late morning
sunshine. She had come here after Daphne Bowler's return from
the police station when the DeLouche party had decided to move
en masse to the city the better to search for Louisa. Cynthia
wanted to have one last taste of this place and rather dreaded their
move to the city, albeit a beautiful Italian city. The farmer with
his little electric train came towards her. She hoped that by sitting
against one of his walnut trees she was not doing anything wrong.
When he came close to her he stopped and the little engine went
past them. He said 'Bon giorno' bowed and gestured for her to
cup her hands together. He reached into his pocket and filled
her hands with walnuts. He said 'mangare' and moved away up
the hill. Cynthia looked at the gift in her hands. The velvet
surface of the outer shells glowed a delicate shade of green. She
pressed her thumbs gently on the curved surfaces and they gave
a little to her touch. Moving her thumbs back and forth she felt
the tiny hairs sweeping one way and then the other. Finally, she
felt for the cleft in the outer shell and prised it away to reveal
the fissures and peaks of the nut. She felt for a stone in the dust
beside her bringing it down firmly and picked the soft fruit out

of its case. She held the walnut to her lips, its leathery surface uneven on her tongue. Biting into the nut, she began to open another one. Chewing walnuts she began to rummage in her bag for her passport. Signor Bignole told her that he had returned it to her already but Cynthia could not remember when. Now she began the search. The bag was made from thick cowhide. Doug Digit had bought it for her in a flea market in Sorcellito when they had gone across the Golden Gate for a day out. It was patched and restitched and grubby but Cynthia liked it. Museum guides and tickets and a torn city map appeared first. Next, came an envelope with a letter reminding her to renew her Amnesty International membership and a letter from the bank about a lost debit card that had somehow got into the same envelope. A nest of blusher, eye liner and lipsticks came next, the crusty surface of a blusher dish crumbling as she tried to revive it. A photograph of her sitting on the steps of her hall of residence surrounded by her students was smeared by an eyeliner sticking to its surface. Cynthia peeled it away and smoothed the photo in her hands. On the back of the picture someone had written 'To darling Mrs D we love you and thanks for all the cakes.' More items appeared, one of which was her passport, and at the bottom a newspaper cutting that gave details of an international conference on climate change and advice about how to reduce carbon footprints. Cynthia remembered she had intended to put it up on the hall noticeboard to encourage her students to do their bit. She had tried to talk to them about the need to save energy but they had seemed blissfully indifferent to the fate of the planet and had taken to calling her 'their eco-warrior' in a gently mocking way clearly intended to give her the responsibility of saving the planet so that they could just get on with enjoying themselves. Cynthia had tried to persuade some of her students to join her the day she went to London to support environmental groups who were demonstrating after the Bali conference but they declined and so she had gone on her own. She recalled arriving at Victoria coach station joining a group of young people who were hand-ing out placards. She chose one that read : 'US – BINDING AGREEMENT – NOW! Standing in Grosvenor Square in front of the embassy felt quite like old times. She marched with a young couple wheeling a push- chair and told them about the day in 1968 at the height of the Vietnam war when there had been another demonstration here and she told them that it was the first war in history that had been stopped by public pressure and the young couple had told her she was an "inspiration" and that they hoped that what they were doing would also change things.

Cynthia folded the newspaper article carefully and put it along with the jumble of items back into her bag. She looked out over the broad plain before her. She could see traffic moving along roads between fields and woods and in the distance an oil refinery its waste chimneys sticking into the sky like organ pipes.

"Penny for them."

"Duncan, I didn't hear you coming."

"Ah, yes. I'm known for my leopard-like movements."

Duncan sat down and let out an 'oof' as he did so.

"You know, I've only recently started to do that."

"What?"

"Go 'oof' when I sit down."

"Too many good lunches, especially here."

"That must be it. Anyway, you're very solitary."

"I wanted to enjoy it all for a bit longer. It's a nuisance really, this Louisa business."

"That's unlike you, Cynthia."

"I know but I was enjoying being back here."

"Back here?"

"Yes Doug and I were here. Years ago."

Duncan knew about Doug Digit and his fatal encounter with the Greyhound bus.

"Love of my life and all that. I sometimes think that being a house-mother is an odd sort of substitution. The students are my 'children on loan' which is great but when I hear them chatting and laughing on the other side of my door I can get very low, lonely."

Duncan stopped himself from saying how the students all loved her and how they were her family and how the college wouldn't know what to do without her.

"There have been others of course, but it's never been the same."

"You've kept that quiet," Duncan said, " But I do remember the enigmatic Mr Lipton."

"Charlie Lipton, yes. Do you know I can't remember where I met him, he just seemed to appear out of nowhere. He was all lavish bouquets and expensive suits, driving me around in his Jensen. He always smelt delicious, some Parisian fragrance. Do you remember when you invited us to dinner, doing your matchmaking bit."

"When he left, he kissed Claire's hand. Very suspect behaviour."

"You were convinced he was a spy."

"No question about it, he was James Bond by another name. A trained killer, Eton, the Guards, a quick interview somewhere in Whitehall and straight into M16."

"It's funny, I've wanted to make things OK with other men but it's never worked out. The sex has been nice, of course, but my heart was never in it and I think they all sensed that. I used to think they just got what they wanted, actually it was me that was rejecting them, not the other way round."

Cynthia turned to look at Duncan who was staring into the distance.

"You're very lucky, having Claire and the children."

"I know."

"You know Pandora's after you."

"Yes, I had noticed. It must be my youthful good looks."

"Be serious, Duncan. You need to be careful."

"I don't think there's anything to be careful about."

"Don't you believe it, there are plenty of women who would jump at you."

"I am not aware of any recent attempts to jump at me."

"I'm not joking. I've seen you at parties – you're always surrounded by women."

"Well, if that is true, it's because I'm safe and besides I like them, prefer them to the company of men mostly."

"Exactly."

"What do you mean?"

"I mean you think everybody has lived in the kind and affectionate world you inhabit with Claire and the children. You listen and reassure and well, comfort us – a strong aphrodisiac for someone who hasn't had much of that, who hasn't been made to feel special.

Anyway, I'm not entirely convinced by this 'What, moi?" act you put on. You work your charm on the good looking Mums who pitch up with their offspring."

"There have been some exotic ones haven't there?"

"Madame Yvenlov, for example. She was practically sitting in your lap when you brought her round to see the house."

"She was fantastic, wasn't she?"

"Yes, wasn't she?"

Cynthia glanced sideways at Duncan and gave him an arch look. He lay back and waited for the moment to pass.

"You're hopeless. But Pandora, seriously, watch out."

"She reads a lot of romantic fiction. Very dangerous."

"You can laugh all you like but this sort of thing happens. Pandora Fulbright has reached the 'now or never' stage, she's away from her mother and knows that this might be her last chance with a man. We're in this romantic place, you're away from your home comforts. Have you noticed how the cardies have given way to slinky dresses?"

"Don't worry, I'm not the affair type. Couldn't do it, even if I wanted to. Not wired that way. All a bit late now anyway. It all looks a bit shabby. I suppose there's some excitement to be had from the secrecy, the thrill of the illicit. But at our age it would be hard to overlook what's really going on."

"In what way?"

"Male menopause, panic in the face of lost youth. All that. Acting out a cliché is never a pretty sight."

The girl in the coffee kiosk rose before him and he felt a sharp twinge of hypocrisy but then dismissed her as harmless fantasy; he knew it was only mental masturbation and like the physical act, had no power beyond itself. As if intuiting his thoughts, Cynthia said:

"It's the difference between F fantasy and PH phantasy."

"Is it?" Duncan said guiltily wondering if he had spoken about the girl out loud by mistake.

"Fantasy is a conscious theatre in which we play out some kind of desire – to fly, to be famous, to have sex with George Clooney or in your case, Claudia Schiffer."

"Thank you, professor. Claudia who, by the way? And the PH phantasy?"

"Ah, now that's different altogether. Phantasy, PH, proceeds from our unconscious mind, from the Id. I like to think of it as the tide which moves beneath the waves of our everyday life."

"I say, that's rather lovely. Tides and waves. Splendid."

"The point is we can't do much about the PH and the F fantasy is just a bit trivial in the end, a bit demeaning and can cause a lot of pain, if its acted out."

"Is this a warning, Mrs Digit? If so you're talking to the wrong person. I know how lucky I am but there's got to be something else, hasn't there?

"Maybe there's nothing else, maybe this is it. Seize the day."

Duncan nodded in the direction of two figures weaving their way through the little terraces and vines that tumbled down the hill to the valley.

"What do you think this is coming up the hill PH or F?"

"Lindsey's just a walking prick."

"Very analytical, Sigmunda. What about the girl?"

"Lucia is lovely but her PH is atavistic. Her tide will make sure that she forgets her summer Englishman and she will marry a lo- cal boy and cut her hair in a sensible bob and have children and become fat and be the holy terror of her husband who will never for a moment think that life can be anything other than what it is."

"I see. Remind me not to look in your crystal ball for myself."

Lindsey and Lucia waved and called 'Ciao.'

"Aha! Director of Studies and housemother in secret love tryst? Do I detect a scandal in the offing," Lindsey said brushing straw and dust from his linen trousers.

Duncan got to his feet and smiled at Lucia.

"Hello you two. Been for a walk?"

"Partly."

Cynthia let out a barely audible snort and said:

"Too much information, Lindsey. Don't you think she's a bit young for you?"

Lucia fiddled with her raven ringlets and moved her weight from one elegant leg to another. She put her hand through Lindsey's arm and said:

"Andiamo. Lo zio ci attende."

"You're as young as you feel, haven't you discovered that yet, Cynthia?"

"Lindsey, we're leaving after lunch. Louisa still hasn't turned up and the police don't seem interested so we're mounting our own investigation."

"I'm sure you don't need me," said Lindsey.

The couple moved on.

"I don't like that man. I'm sure he's a risk to our students. Some of them are only sixteen."

"He's a good tutor. Did you know he could speak Russian? I saw him having a long chat with Ivan's father." Duncan said.

"That's three things he's good at then."

Duncan and Cynthia climbed the terraces and emerged onto the piazza as the campanile bells tolled twelve. Signor Bignole greeted them and ushered them into the dining room.

"You have chosen the right transport for your holiday, signore y signorina The petrol shortage is beginning to spread. My cousin closed his filling station yesterday – no more gasoline. The summer trade is not so good. The hotel across the square has already cancellations."

CHAPTER 21

LOUISA AND UTTER HAD spent the night wandering the city. Utter had told Louisa that he had nowhere to stay and that anyway, the best time to see the city was at night. So they had walked. They went past cafes and bars with the last customers standing on pavements deciding which way to go home as tired barmen closed shutters and brought in empty glasses and swept cigarette ash into gutters. They stood by fountains and felt the cool purity of water running through their hands and sat on stone benches in a park beneath plane trees and made patterns with their feet in the dust. They went around the circle of benches and made a new pattern at each bench. Moving on, they found two tiny gloves on some metal railings and Louisa put them on one finger of each hand and made up a puppet show for Utter who gasped and cried and laughed in all the right places. They stood by a church with a domed roof and looked up and were amazed at the little figure that turned in the night breeze. The figure stood on one leg, the other being bent in movement. It held a sail attached to a delicate mast and gallant and it was this sail that caused the figure to rotate in the breeze. The mast and the sail and the figure were of gold and seemed to be on fire as the moonlight caught its surfaces until Louisa and Utter said that it was liquid and had no substance beyond light and movement. Later they had come out of their reverie and made up a game in which there was a penalty each time one of them trod on moonlight and the penalties were silly and they laughed at each other's inability to stand on one leg or balance twigs on their noses. And coming out of a narrow street a police car had slowed and the driver had eyed them suspiciously and when it had gone Utter had performed a mime in which he was arrested and thrown into a deep dungeon. And Louisa wept for him and came at night, Houdini like with a key in her throat and crept past the guards and released him and they had run away. In all of this long night together there had been none of the banal interrogation of what and who and where. Just before dawn they had sat together looking up at the sky as it paled into light and then around them at the empty street and he had asked her how she felt. Louisa had thought for a little and then said 'free' and she had taken his hand in hers but he had withdrawn from her and she had asked him what the matter was and he had shrugged and said nothing.

*

Louisa rested the laminated sign that read 'Da Vinci : Toilets' against the wall of the Chiesa San Martine and called to Utter.

"Is this OK?"

Utter was busy setting up a series of small objects that fanned out from a pale blue toilet seat that was raised from the ground on four bricks. A fifth brick was placed in the middle of the seat with the word 'Relief' written on it. The exhibition was being set up in the narrow alley running along the West wall of the church.

"Good. We are almost ready."

"We need to make a roof for our gallery."

Utter produced a white sheet and a lump hammer from his back-pack and hammered the sheet into place above the exhibits. He stretched the sheet across the narrow alley and created the desired canopy.

"How will we get people to come?"

"I have a little piece of marketing that will work."

Utter held up a billboard on which he had written:

This Is Crap, Come See It.

Admission Free. Donations Welcome

"Very inviting."

"It's always worked before. You'd be surprised."

Louisa smiled at her new friend with his spiky hair and pointed shoes and fairy tale appearance.

"Cool."

The whole exhibition was set out on an enormous velvet blanket pulled into peaks and ridges to separate the exhibits into sections at the centre of which was the toilet seat. In the first section a crushed mineral bottle was rammed into a length of pipe at the other end of which was an ornamental tap; next was a balloon attached by a colourful tassle that Louisa thought she recognized, this had been secured to the ground by a pair of bellows; in the next section three fire alarm covers were placed in a circle of velvet hills; finally the delicate skull of a mouse was placed on the top of a small mound of earth, a worm just visible beneath the soil as it fell away.

"They are all from the exhibition."

"Even the mouse?"

"Even the mouse."

"You were hard at work."

"What do you think?"

"I think it's… I don't know."

"Good, that's the first step," he said.

Utter took off his glasses and wiped them on his shirt sleeve. Louisa recognized this as a sign that Utter was about to make a statement.

"The point is people need to think. When they see things in galleries it helps them not to think. You go to a gallery and you are already expecting certain things, cultural signifiers, referencing that robs the work of its energy, its life. I want people to see things differently, surprise them."

Utter looked around at his exhibits.

"We have transformed these things just by giving them a different context."

"Cool."

" Well, shall we open?"

An hour later there was a respectable heap of Euros in their donations box and Utter declared the exhibition a success. He was pleased by the public's response. One viewer had been irritated by "this pile of junk" others amused by what they saw as the ironies in the exhibition. Utter had argued with a group of German tourists about aesthetics and Louisa had watched it all and been amazed at the strong feelings that Utter's 'work' produced.

"Time to go – before the police move us on."

They gathered up the four corners of the velvet blanket and gently pulled them together to make a sack.

Utter and Louisa sat drinking a beer and watching a group of Japanese tourists coming out of a Venetian mask shop wearing their purchases.

"Weird."

"Yes. Utter, I think I'd better go now."

"Go where?"

"Back. They'll be wondering where I am."

Louisa felt suddenly depressed by the thought of her mother and the collective disapproval of the DeLouche cycling party that would await her on her return.

"Please yourself. Don't think I will be stopping you. You can go whenever you like. Just go."

"Utter, what's wrong?"

"Nothing."

"We can see each other, but I just need to go back and tell them I'm OK."

"Yes, yes. Go back to Mummy. So much for feeling free."

"Utter. That's unfair. It's been cool."

"Cool, cool. Why go back to them? What have they done for you – apart from making you scared."

"Scared?"

"Scared to be yourself."

" I can be myself but she's my mother, she'll be worried about me."

"Worried she'll have to think who she is if she hasn't got you around."

"Utter, I don't understand. Why are you so angry? Utter?"

Utter was staring past Louisa at a newsstand.

"My God."

"What?"

"Your present. It wasn't a mock-up. There's a reward for its recovery. The police are looking for the thief. They're looking for me. Look there's a picture of my banner."

The newspaper article reported the theft from Da Vinci's notebook accompanied by a picture of the Museum, the words on Utter's banner clearly visible in the background.

"It says that two pages were taken."

"Two? But you only gave me one."

"I only took one."

"It must have been someone who knew they were real."

A suspicion crossed Louisa's mind – what if Utter knew they were real as well? Had he planted the other one on her? Was she being used as a carrier?

"We can just go to the police and hand it in, or leave it somewhere and contact them, tell them where it is," Louisa said.

Utter seemed to consider this and then said:

"Maybe."

"This is scary now. Do the police know what you look like?"

"No, why should they?" Utter took off his glasses and cleaned his lenses on his sleeve. Louisa took the page from her pocket, laid it carefully in her sketch pad and said:

"Let's go."

Chapter 22

The distinctive colours of the Two Wheels Good bicycles – blue, yellow and green slashed over the ovoid frames and woven into bulging panniers – were clearly visible on the bikes stacked together beneath the plane trees of the Montepuliano town square. Daphne Bowler and her group had stopped for something to eat on their way to the city where they hoped to find Louisa. The piazza was arranged along the length of what remained of the castle wall and formed a long rectangle bordered by fifty two trees. Beneath the trees stone benches were interspersed with swan necked lampposts holding aloft large opaque orbs. Here and there ladders leaned against the trees, their upper ends disappearing into leafy interiors. Men stood on the bottom rung of each ladder and looked up to where disembodied hands could be seen snipping leaf and twig and responding to the guidance and instructions offered from below.

Steve Durrant emerged from an alimentare and looked along the length of the trees. He saw that each one of them had been shaped to resemble World War Two German helmets. He crossed the road to one of the stone benches where Pandora Fulbright was peeling greased paper away from a slim packet of sliced proscuitto.

"Mind if I join you, Pandora?"

"Steve, of course. You can have some of this."

"Only if you accept some of my salami in exchange."

They set about breaking bread and feeding the wafer thin meats into the split rolls they held in the palms of their hands.

"And what does the Lonely Planet say about these then Pandora?"

Steve jerked his head in the direction of the trees.

"They are a memorial to the townspeople who were killed here in the war. There are fifty two trees representing fifty two people the Germans shot as a reprisal. There was a lot of resistance activity in the hills here during the war. They were very successful at disrupting transport, blowing up switching stations and so on. The Germans finally took action, rounded men up at random and shot them. Over there."

Pandora indicated a round flower bed at one end of the piazza. At the centre of the bed was a plaque bearing the fifty two names and some pictures of the victims behind glass that had become discoloured by weather and time.

"Sad. Seems a bit odd to make these helmet shapes," Steve said.

"They didn't want anyone to forget who had done this, I suppose."

"It was a memorial that turned me on to classics, in Greece."

"Really. Tell me."

"I was with my parents and my two sisters. My Dad was a teacher and we used to spend every summer rolling about Peloponnisos or Sterea Ellas in a battered old Morris Minor. How we ever got it to go that far every summer I shall never know. Anyway, we were on our way to Piraeus from Lamia to get the boat out to the islands and the road went past this enormous monument."

"Thermopylae."

"Yes, how did you know?"

"It's the only one on that road."

"Right. Anyway, I looked at this socking great thing and screamed at my Dad to stop. It was magnificent. About forty yards long and twenty feet high and just there by the road surrounded by nothing, miles of open Greek country- side. It had a stepped top and right on the final surface ...."

"A Spartan soldier."

"Yes, and the size of him. Majestic. Huge, muscular legs encased in greaves, chest broad and flat against the sun, his head thrown back with a helmet that seemed literally to be made of gold. His arm was behind him gripping a spear. I jumped out of the car with everyone complaining that it was too hot to stop in the middle of the day and shouting at me to get back in so we could get a breeze going again. And my Dad saying 'no let the lad look'. And I looked and looked and I couldn't decide if the Spartan was wounded and dying or whether he was pulling back before launching his spear at the Persians. Of course, I didn't know about Leonidas and the four hundred Spartans or Xerxes' army then. All I knew was that this thing ...."

Steve opened and closed his hands as if he were trying to gather words in to explain what he meant.

"Had meaning for you," Pandora said.

"Yes, that's it. Had meaning. After a bit my Dad came over and told me about how the Spartans had held off the Persians, even though they were outnumbered. And here's the thing. When Dad pulled back onto the road I looked out of the rear window at the monument and a boy, about my age, was leaning against the foot of the statue. He pulled out a set of pan-pipes and began to play them – I could just hear them above the noise of the engine. He was stripped to the waist and as he played goats came out from behind the monument and started to graze at its base. They must have come out of the field behind"

"Quite a moment."

"Yes. I can remember it as if it were yesterday. But you know the place."

"Yes, I was there. Years ago. I hitch-hiked along that road. I was glad of the monument. It gave me shade while I waited for my next lift."

"Right. I didn't think of you as much of a traveller."

"I don't travel much now."

Steve offered Pandora a little plastic tub of olives.

"Your mother will be missing you," he said.

"Yes, she will."

Pandora knew that her mother would not be missing her; would not, in fact, ever miss her again.

"She'll enjoy your postcards though."

"Yes."

Pandora thought about the weeks leading up to the holiday. Her mother had seemed to go into a decline as soon as she knew Pandora was going away. She began to complain about chest pains or said that her eyes were getting very bad and when Pandora came home from teaching she would find her leaning against the banisters or peering very closely at unopened envelopes. Pandora could not tell whether her mother really was 'worse' or whether she was putting on an act to make her daughter feel guilty. Long evenings in the gloom of their little front room with Mrs Fulbright's skeletal face inches from the TV screen and the volume turned up so loud that the neighbours had banged on the party wall had taken their toll. It was at times like this that Pandora had wanted her mother to die, had wanted her not to be there so that she could have a life. But what life? Her mother and looking after her mother was her life, had been her life for so long that she was not sure she could live any other way. And then the day when she had come home and turned the key in the front door and noticed the garish colours on the parquet flooring of the hall thrown by the stained glass panels in the door and listened for the domestic sounds that would locate her mother. And her hearing nothing and calling "Mother, Mother" and moving from room to room and beginning to feel sick (a feeling that would not leave her for days after) and climbing the stairs and noticing the threadbare treads and not wanting to go any further but going further and all the while calling and falling away in her mind so that when she opened the bedroom door and saw her mother lying straight on the candlewick cover of her bed, her housecoat neatly folded over her thin body and the soles of the slippers Pandora had bought her for Christmas facing her like two little tombstones she did not feel relieved, or guilty or anything. The days that followed seemed to be an acting out of actions she had rehearsed in her mind in preparation for this time. Now the moment had come, burdened with guilt and sorrow, there seemed to be two Pandoras moving through the hours: one who was dealing with funeral arrangements and making decisions about the order of service with the vicar and her mother's will; and another Pandora who had been stopped in her tracks while normality went on, oblivious to the blinding grief that held her like a child who waits to be picked up and comforted.

"She's gone."

"Who?"

"Mother. She died before we left England."

"But the postcards."

"I needed to send them."

Steve sat for a moment without saying anything.

"I understand," Steve said.

"Do you? It sounds daft, doesn't it? Sending postcards to someone who's dead. But it helped, in a way. I can't really remember a time when I wasn't looking after her. And I always sent her cards, took pictures. Death's a funny business isn't it? I mean, I know she's not physically here but she's still with me. It's as if lives have a momentum that carries them beyond death. That's how it's felt and I suppose being away has made it easier to maintain the illusion. I think I've been in shock. I haven't been able to accept that she's dead."

"I can understand. After so long. It must be hard."

"Thank you. I haven't told anyone else."

Pandora and Steve finished their picnic and waved to the other members of the DeLouche cycling party who had sauntered into the piazza seeking the cool shade of the trees and who sat about on separate benches. The pruning team finished their work and came down the ladders. There was an air of reverence about the way they moved, lowering the ladders and packing away shears in canvas bags that they shouldered leaving a free hand to carry other implements or the end of a ladder. They formed up in a loose column and came past the benches and their conversation was muted and heavy with the memory of what had happened a lifetime ago.

Dear Wrinklies

Sonny and I in Jakarta. Hot. Spent some time with a man called Benny from West Guinea. He was a community leader but had to leave his village. The authorities suppressing his people. He told us about the logging companies stripping his ancestral lands and moving people out of the area. I got a bit worried about talking to him – all very political. He asked for help. We said we'd tell people about it all when we got home then we managed to get away from him. Sonny suffering from an exploding bum, we're running out of immodium but I think there's enough to bung him up. Big cockroaches here – they eat each other.

Love Simon

Simon Yoot

Good call on ditching the freedom fighter. Bit too real. Renew Amnesty membership best thing. They also serve etc, etc. Hope Sonny now sorted out. Take care of yourself.

Love Dad

Chapter 23

THE LOGGIA OF THE Palazzo Bignole, owned and run by Signor Bignole's brother Fabio, is a very pleasant place to be. Apart from the shade it provides to those lounging on the curved opulence of the rattan chairs, it is a vantage point from which to see the city. Looking westward the Duomo can be glimpsed at the far end of the Via Sebastian and the marble façade of the Doge's winter quarters is visible above the shallow roofs of the Pianta district. An observer, trailing his or her hand along the red stone of the balustrade and arriving at the east end of the loggia is treated to the sight of the twelfth century Chiesa San Spirito which contains a triptych by Buoninsegna. If the eyesight of the onlooker is acute and they have long enough to stand and stare they will notice that the campanile has two clock faces one with the correct time and one an hour and a half out. This second time setting is for the devil, who, it was felt by the founding fathers of the modern city, needed to be combated in as many ways as possible. The interior of the loggia is decorated with tempera depicting mythical scenes, female figures dance with satyrs beneath trees dripping with figs and pomegranates, the faded colours interrupted here and there with patches of plaster where the surface has blistered and burst and been repaired.

Daphne Bowler stood with her hands clamped on the balustrade and looked out at the city like a general surveying the battleground. She was reassuring herself that Louisa was out there somewhere and that it was just a matter of organizing a methodical search to find her. Caught between anxiety for her lost child and anger that Louisa was, once again, the cause of difficulty and complication, Daphne drummed her fingers on the warm stone and remembered another time when her offspring had gone missing. She had been working as a broker in the heady days of the eighties, before city bonuses were dirty words and when barrow boys and trust fund yuppies raised glasses of Chardonnay in chrome lined bars. She left Louisa in the ground floor crèche ('Tiny Tots – Caring for the Working Day') before taking the lift to the eighteenth floor of the Canary Wharf office where she worked. One day she was calculating projections for Rio Tinto Zinc and had been interrupted by the appearance of Belinda, all Alice band and Laura Ashley, who had taken the lift to tell her that they could not find Louisa. There was a flurry of activity that included the arrival of a Panda car and the office security man who had assured Daphne, rather unconvincingly, that Louisa could not have gone far and that it would all be all right. A little group of Tiny Tots' staff then fanned out along Marsh Wall while Daphne was given a stiff drink and awaited news. After forty minutes of queasy anticipation and another stiff drink, Louisa appeared led by Belinda, her Alice band slightly askew. The four year old had been found sitting on a bar stool being fed crepes by the owner of the South Quay Sandwich Bar who had noticed the little girl sauntering along the pavement without appearing to be attached to any of the other pedestrians. Daphne smacked the loggia wall and shook this memory away. A hand was laid on her back and Cynthia was beside her.

"Hello, my dear. How are you?" Cynthia asked.

"Keen to get on. I've asked Inspector Grippe to drop in and give us an update and maybe a steer on how to go about the search. Here he is now."

The two women watched as a dark blue Alfa Romeo drew up opposite the Palazzo Bignole. Inspector Grippe and another man emerged from the car.

"Look, it's Lindsey. What on earth is he doing with the Italian Police?"

As if Lindsey had heard Cynthia he glanced up at the loggia, moved away along the Via Sebastian and was lost among the mid-morning shoppers.

"How very odd."

Cynthia's enjoyment of this little mystery was brought to an abrupt halt as her eyes focused on the figure of Inspector Grippe crossing the road and disappearing through the Palazzo entrance below the loggia. By the time she was looking down on the bald patch on the crown of the inspector's head Cynthia knew that she had seen a ghost.

"Cynthia, whatever is it?"

Daphne Bowler prevented Cynthia from dashing her head on the stone floor as she fell in a faint by grabbing her under the arms and swinging her onto one of the rattan chairs. Daphne fanned her client's ashen face and limp body and wondered what could have brought on this sudden loss of consciousness. The day was not unusually hot and they had recently finished a pasta lunch washed down by a modest quantity of Chianti. Dismissing either of these explanations as unlikely she got to work.

"Let's get the blood flowing in the right direction."

Daphne raised Cynthia's sandalled feet above the level of her head hoping this would aid recovery. Cynthia's body began to shake.

"Oh, Christ we've got a fitter."

Deciding this might be a correct diagnosis, and preparing for the grim business of fishing Cynthia's tongue out of her mouth, Daphne turned her patient into the recovery position and waited. The oak door that let onto the upper gallery of the Palazzo creaked open and Inspector Grippe appeared breathing heavily from the exertion of climbing two flights of stairs. Ignoring Daphne Bowler he stood over the prone figure. Cynthia's eyelids fluttered, came to rest, fluttered again and finally opened.

"Doug?"

"Cynthia?"

"You're dead"

"No, I'm alive."

Daphne was thoroughly confused by this exchange which seemed to indicate that these two people had fallen into a state of idiocy. Since neither of them were taking any notice of her, and seeing that Cynthia had regained full consciousness albeit at the expense of her reason, she left the loggia to them.

"You're a police inspector."

"Yes."

"With the Italian police."

"More or less."

"More or less?"

"It's hard to explain."

"I would imagine it is."

"Yes, look, perhaps …"

Cynthia struggled into the upright position and propelled herself to her feet. Her head swam and she sat down again abruptly.

"You've had a shock. You need to lie down," he said.

"No, I'm OK. I'll sit here. I can't believe this. What are you doing here?"

Cynthia held up her hand.

"I mean apart from being an Italian policeman. How did you get here? Why are you here? What does all this mean …?"

"It's great to see you."

"What, what? What do you mean 'it's great to see me?'"

Cynthia's voice became hysterical in the face of this banal compliment, as if they had not seen each other for months rather than half a lifetime.

"OK, OK. Let me explain."

Doug Digit, aka Inspector Giuseppe Grippe lit a cigarette, gathered himself and began.

CHAPTER 24

"I GUESS THE FIRST thing to say is about Mom and Dad. I think I told you they were dead. They weren't dead. They lived at Blackpoint – at the end of the bay but by the time I met you I was already working undercover and hadn't been home for quite a while."

"Undercover?"

"I was monitoring demonstrations, collecting information on known antiwar agitators."

"For whom?"

"The CIA."

Cynthia's mental landscape, the geology of memory and belief, underwent a second tremor. The tectonic plates on which she had founded her life were, she felt, about to undergo further shifts.

"Go on."

"Look, I know all of this is going to be difficult …. Anyway, I managed to infiltrate one group who we were interested in, I'd been at Berkeley with some of them and they trusted me. Once they had been lifted …"

"Lifted?"

"These were early days but I guess it was a kind of internal rendition that allowed us to remove people, for questioning, to … detain those who were a threat."

"A threat?"

"Yes, national security was being compromised. Public opinion was turning against the war. It had to be … dealt with."

Cynthia turned the silver bracelets on her wrist. This was a double betrayal. The long years since Cynthia had lost Doug had been made bearable partly by the memory of his passion for civil rights and his participation in anti-war demonstrations. In memory of Doug she had joined Amnesty and she felt that his spirit had been with her in London on the day she marched against the Iraq War. And now she learned that he had been the enemy all the time, part of the ill defined 'them' who did unspeakable things in the name of security and freedom while all the time merely maintaining power and influence over weaker states.

"After that my work was done. It was around the time of the Tete offensive and the CIA were getting more involved on the ground in Vietnam. I was assigned to one of the reconnaissance groups operating in the south but first I had to disappear so the Greyhound crash was arranged."

"But why, why couldn't you just go?"

She experienced a series of mental images of herself – at the hospital unable to face identifying the body; at the graveside with a token representative from Berkeley; reading a condolence note from their landlord.

"The CIA likes to make its stories convincing, if you see what I mean."

Cynthia failed to see what he meant but said nothing. She was thinking about the young man she had known – or not known. And how was she ever going to reconcile the CIA agent with her sandy haired lover who had sat on Turkish cushions in their joss stick scented room in Height Ashbury and railed against the Republican bully boys.

"Soon after that I was in Tay Ninh, South Vietnam. I was there for a year, working alongside local recruits, moving around the villages, picking up any suspects and shipping them on to Saigon. We were pretty effective. I had to get used to wearing black pyjamas and carrying an M16 and being kept up at night by insects and rats. We moved in, got who we wanted and moved out, mostly people didn't even know we were there."

Doug drew a hand through his thinning hair and looked at Cynthia.

"Perhaps you don't want to know all this."

"I need to know it, Doug, I have to know it. I don't know what I'm going to do with it all, but I must know it."

Something had to fill the void that Doug was opening up with every sentence he uttered, a new set of waymarks were needed to populate her internal landscape, to give this wasteland shape, bitter though it would be.

"I was with the unit for a year before my accident. I broke my leg – in three places. It's full of titanium pins. If you want to know when it's going to rain ask me."

When Doug looked at Cynthia and smiled she looked away from him. She couldn't imagine a situation in which she would be asking him anything. He realized that it was too soon to try and win her back, too soon to receive absolution and so he went on with his story.

"We'd been to a village – Phan Hua it was called – to pick up a guy who we knew was moving small arms around the district and stirring up resistance. Anyway, this guy took us into the village, pointed out the hut where our man was sleeping and let us do the rest. The thing about it was the man in question was a boy of about seven or eight years old. He was kind of hard to hang on to and keep quiet. We got him back to the Jeep and were just moving off when he threw himself onto the road and ran for it. My driver tried to cut him off but the front wheel hit a rock and we turned over. I was thrown out and the Jeep landed on top of me. That was the end of my time with the unit.

Despite herself, Cynthia found herself asking why.

"We weren't supposed to go on operations with the Vietnamese so when this was written up in the report I was quietly moved on."

As he spoke Cynthia began to see the young man again. The thinning hair and sagging cheeks gave way to a blonde mop and the chiselled filmstar jaw line that Cynthia remembered. The beginnings of forgiveness were here too, although Cynthia would not recognize this until later.

"Did you come home then?"

"Yes."

"Did you ever think of me?"

"It's complicated."

"You lied to me. You were lying to me all the time. Your whole life was a lie. My God, you were good at it. I never suspected. Never. I loved you."

"We had some good times together. You were my English rose."

"I thought you were dead."

"I missed you. I kept your picture."

"I believed in you."

Their words petered out and they fell into silence. Cynthia felt that finding Doug again and hearing about the life he had led could only be thought about obliquely, such was its power like a tidal tsunami to sweep her away altogether.

"And after?"

"I went back once more. At the end, to get our people out. When Siagon fell. The photograph of the helicopter on the roof of the American embassy?"

Cynthia nodded numbly.

"I was there. You can just make me out behind the line of people going up."

"Bully for you."

"After that I was assigned to Iran. When the Shah went into exile in '79 I stayed on. They were bad years. By '81 our people had been allowed to go home. I worked with the Mujahadein when the Russians occupied Afghanistan but by the end of the eighties things were changing and I'd had enough, I requested a transfer to Europe and was given a new cover. It took a long time to get the accent out of my Italian. People think I'm from Calabria now. I haven't been used much in recent years but things are on the move again. The new Russia and all. The old bear is flexing his muscles again. This oil business. Georgia…

"And has there been anyone, is there anyone? I'm sorry, perhaps I don't have a right to ask. We've both had another life since then," Cynthia said.

"It's OK. And, no, there wasn't anyone for a long time after you. But I'm settled now. I have an apartment near the Duomo. I see someone, every so often. A local woman. We met in a bar. It makes things ... easier."

"Yes. Well. Why was Lindsey in your car when you arrived?"

"Who? You know him."

"Of course, I do. We're here together."

"Together?"

"No not together, together. He's in our group."

"Who are you working for?"

"Look, stop this. Lindsey is a tutor in the tutorial college I work for. We're all here on a cycling holiday."

"Right. Look Cynthia. Could we keep this conversation to ourselves for the moment. And could you forget that you saw me with .... Lindsey. It's quite important."

"Whatever you say, Inspector. There is something you should know before I put Doug out of my mind again. I had a child, we had a child. A boy."

"I know."

CHAPTER 25

LOUISA HAD ABANDONED HER thoughts about returning to her mother, partly because she did not know where her mother was and partly because she had been stung by Utter's accusation that she was scared of being herself. If she had been scared at all, it was of him. She had been shocked by the way his cool detachment had suddenly turned to anger. Afterwards he had said he was sorry, that he did not know what had come over him and she had forgiven him and so she had stayed with him. Utter had agreed to go to the police with the Da Vinci page and this, too, had made Louisa feel better.

"It's nice without the traffic, isn't it? Louisa said.

"It's spooky – like something from a science fiction film."

They stood on a deserted street corner wondering which direction to take while the nearby traffic lights signalled red to green and back again to an empty road. Across the street a chain had been looped across the entrance to a filling station and a large improvised sign read CHIUSO.

"Do you know where we are?"

"No," Utter said.

"It's great this."

"What is great?"

"Well just this. I don't know where I am and I don't know where I'm going. Usually, I'd be in a panic but this is different. It's great."

"I thought you wanted to get back. To your Mum and everyone."

"Yeah, well."

Satisfied that this was an adequate answer, Louisa sat down on the pavement and reached into a canvas bag that was slung over her shoulder. Selecting a piece of charcoal from her Pocahontas pencil case, she began to sketch a cat that appeared from across the street and was now curled at her feet. Looking up from the page where a swirling outline was taking shape she stared at the strip of blue sky visible between the buildings along the road.

"Hot, isn't it?"

"Umm."

Utter pushed the thick black rims of his glasses onto the bridge of his nose.

"I don't steal things, you know. Taking things from fat cat galleries – that's not stealing."

"It's OK. When we find a police station it'll all be OK."

A black limousine, the driver and passenger barely visible behind smoked glass, cruised up the street and stopped opposite Louisa and Utter. For a moment there was no movement and then the passenger door opened and a man emerged, his bullet head accentuated by a severe crew cut. Louisa looked up from her drawing and took in the pasty, pockmarked face of Colonel Smirka. She stared at him trying to remember where she had seen this man before and, failing to do so, began to sketch his face next to the cat. The Russian moved towards a cigarette machine on the petrol station forecourt. Returning to the car he leant his arms on the roof of the limousine and tore away the cellophane wrapping jumping a cigarette out of the packet. He seemed in no hurry, taking long pulls and looking up and down the street, as if he were waiting for someone. When he noticed the two young people, his mood changed. He flicked the cigarette away from him and disappeared into the shaded interior of the limousine. The vehicle moved away.

"I knew that man. Look."

Louisa showed Utter her sketch, the sagging features and pitted surface of the Colonel's face faithfully represented, the flicking tail of the cat appearing to give him a horn protruding from the top of his head.

"I've got it. He was at the college, when I went for my interview. Cool. I remembered. What's he doing here? He didn't look as if he was on holiday."

Louisa took the Da Vinci page from her pad. She looked at the mirror writing.

"Look, these letters are the right way round, they've been added. They're newer. Look. TOS. What does it mean?"

Any further thoughts about the meaning of this discovery were swept away by the sudden appearance of Louisa's mother astride her bike at the end of the street. Before she had time to see the fugitive pair they had retreated into the shade of the petrol station forecourt. They watched as Daphne Bowler wheeled past them.

"Hey, that's a bit of luck. Look what I've found."

CHAPTER 26

"A TANDEM! JUST WHAT we need," said Louisa.

Louisa had nearly hailed her mother as she went past but she was having an adventure and it was not quite time to give it up. The appearance of the mystery Russian and the discovery on Da Vinci's page was too exciting to merely hand over to the adults.

"Come on, Utter. Let's go."

As they wheeled onto the street they heard three voices shouting Louisa's name. Turning to look, Louisa saw her housemother, the Director of Studies and the Classic tutor red faced and waving frantically. Louisa's pedals took on a life of their own as Utter pushed forward. Picking up speed Utter changed gears and Louisa had to hang on tightly to her handle bars.

"Tell me when you're going to do that," she said.

"Sorry, but you must keep up with me. Lean into this corner."

The elongated bike clipped the edge of the pavement and then was round the corner, the pursuing bikes temporarily losing sight of them, their shouted order to stop being lost as the tandem sped past some workmen holding a chute that was disgorging rubble into a skip.

Louisa looked behind just in time to see their pursuers dodging lumps of masonry being sprayed across the road from the chute, the workmen having briefly lost control of it. The luckless trio emerged from a cloud of dust, coughing and blinking. The road ahead was clear but as they reached the next junction the galleon figure of Daphne Bowler sailed into their path and stopped. Utter, who was thoroughly enjoying the chase, summoned up more strength and swerved past the immobile mother. Louisa, head lowered and pedalling hard looked up from her exertions and saw the enraged, purple face of her mother at close quarters before they whipped past her.

Looking ahead Louisa could not work out why the road came to an end with nothing but blue sky beyond it. As they neared this void they slowed to take in the situation. The front wheel of the tandem rested on the top step of a wide set of stairs connecting the upper and lower town. With their pursuers now in clear view behind them, they realized that it was time for desperate measures.

"Hold on," Utter shouted.

Pointing the tandem at the smooth drain track running down the middle of the stairway, Utter strove to keep the front wheel away from the steps. Late morning shoppers coming up the steps were annoyed, amused and frightened by the riders so that, as they veered downwards, Louisa seemed to be looking at live gargoyles moving past her. Mrs Bowler had now joined forces with the others and, having failed to stop at the top of the stairs, all four riders were careering pell-mell downwards, their jerking and erratic movements scattering the alarmed pedestrians. Shopping bags were hurled aside in the melee, melons and oranges rolling and bursting down the steps. One unfortunate man leaping from foot to foot in the path of the oncoming Classics tutor, jumped the wrong way at the last moment and was scooped onto the front mudguard from whence he instinctively embraced the rider. There followed a brief struggle between them, the rider trying to gain forward vision, the reluctant passenger merely trying to avoid falling backwards and thereby becoming a victim beneath the very wheels that supported him. Realising that their only salvation lay in teamwork they settled into an equitable shape, the head of the hapless local tucked into the chest of the Englishman. Utter and Louisa had now reached the bottom of the stairs and immediately set about making good their escape. The others arrived at the horizontal soon after and were surrounded by those whose life and limb they had threatened. There seemed to be no hard feelings and spontaneous applause greeted them. Hands were shaken, the remains of the morning shopping retrieved,

Steve and his passenger embraced each other warmly and the DeLouche search party set off once more.

Taking another corner Utter and Louisa were confronted by an enormous crucifix followed by a swaying statue of the Virgin Mary mounted on a float and being carried by men dressed in ecclesiastical robes. The tail end of the tandem swung out as they applied the brakes so that Louisa was nearly catapulted into the oncoming crowd. They dismounted and squeezed along the side of the procession that filled the entire width of the street. The air was thick from incense emanating from the ornamental thuribles swung by young acolytes. Three bikes were now visible above the heads of the crowd as the DeLouche party held their machines aloft and waded into the devotional crowd. Occasionally one of them would dip and disappear to re-emerge some yards later breasting the tide and making slow forward progress. At one point one of the bikes was adorned by a Cardinal's hat but this was briskly retrieved and returned to its owner, the English tones of the Director of Studies clearly audible – "Sorry, sorry, excuse me madam". There was a spontaneous chorus from an Ave Verum that Louisa had time to note was rather lovely before the press of the crowd became too much and Utter steered the tandem into an open doorway.

They found themselves in the front room of a dwelling. A large table was set with food and, at the head of the table, an ancient crone stood with a crystal goblet full to the brim with red wine. At her side was a tall man dressed in reverential black. Before Utter could give his apologies for their intrusion, the old lady raised her glass, said "Please. sit", and beckoned them to high backed chairs. Had they not known better they might have thought they had wondered onto the set of a Fellini flm. As it was, they merely stared at their hostess and did as they were told. Louisa forgot Utter's flash of temper and her doubts over the theft and, tucking into a delicious antipasta, declared that this was by far the very coolest thing that had happened to her. Utter pointed to the dish in front of him and grinned at their hostess.

"Carciofi giardiniera sono saporiti. Deliziosi."

The old lady fell back in her chair the effort of enunciating the name of the dish seeming to overwhelm her.

"Come ti chiami?"

They told her their names with mouths full and then asked hers.

"Mi chiamo Contessa Spaggia."

The wild laughter that followed this announcement was unsettling. Utter looked closely at his next forkful and hoped that there was no family connection with the Borgias. The primi piatti that followed – a bread gnocchi in broth – was enlivened by a bottle of Virello 89 dispatched with indecent haste. The Contessa nodded at her young guests and clapped her hands in encouragement as one course followed another served by the sepulchral butler. Agnello all'araba was placed before them with vegetables that had surely been gathered that morning from the salad garden Louisa could see through the glazed door behind their hostess.

"You are very kind, Contessa. There are many places set here, were you expecting others today? enquired Utter.

"No, solo voi. Only you."

Louisa shrugged her shoulders quite happy to accept the situation. She glanced at Utter and attributed this latest surprise to him, after all since they had met her life had been full of surprises. She didn't think he had arranged this feast but began to think that somehow these sort of things just happened to him. After a plate of amaretti fritters, the diners rose from the table, icing sugar from their 'dolce' flecking their chins, thanked their hostess, remounted their tandem and rode it out of the room and into the full glare of an Italian afternoon. The street was empty now, the procession had returned the Virgin Mary to her place in the local church, the vestments had been folded away for another year and the commune officials had returned home to sit in their vests in front of the TV.

Hoping that the chase had gone cold, Utter and Louisa found a piazza shaded by trees and lay down and fell asleep; the wine, the food, the furious pedalling and the heat of the day combining to lull them into a deep sleep.

CHAPTER 27

Inspector Grippe stood over the sleeping figures and congratulated himself that, in finding them, he had solved several problems at one stroke. He would be able to return the errant daughter to her mother, arrest the art thief and recover the stolen property. So much for his civil duties as a member of the Italian police force. There would be other benefits to this meeting. He shook Utter's shoulder.

"Utter Hoppe?"

"Yes. Who are you?"

"Inspector Giuseppe Grippe."

He flashed his warrant card at Utter.

"Who is your companion?"

"Louisa."

Louisa rubbed her eyes and sat up.

"Bowler, I'm Louisa Bowler."

"Your mother has been looking for you."

"I know. We saw her this morning. Briefly."

Louisa could not resist a smile as she remembered the fleeting image of her furious mother.

"Well, I will take you to her in due course. There are other matters to be dealt with. Utter Hoppe I am arresting you for damaging public property, causing a public nuisance, and removing exhibits from the city museum."

"Exhibit. I only took one and I didn't know what I was taking."

"Exhibit, then. I can either take you down to the station and charge you or we can come to another arrangement."

"What other arrangement, what for?"

"Show me the page."

Louisa gave the page to the inspector.

"What are you offering us?"

"A great deal to you. Have you ever been in an Italian prison? Look, you don't know … this could be dangerous … for both of you."

Louisa thought that the fun part of her holiday might be coming to an abrupt and unpleasant end.

"We were on our way to hand the page in," Louisa said.

What followed happened so quickly that Louisa hardly had time to catch her breath before it was all over. The first thing she was aware of was being jostled aside by rough hands. She saw Utter turn to catch her and his glasses falling off.

"Lindsey! What are you doing?"

Lindsey North had appeared from nowhere and was now wrestling with Inspector Grippe. At first the younger man got the upper hand but the bulky figure of the inspector was able to press his assailant back and pin him over a bench. Louisa looked around for help but the piazza was deserted. She sprang on the figure of Lindsey but was knocked aside by a flailing arm. Utter was on his hands and knees feeling the ground for his glasses. Lindsey struck the Inspector who fell backwards throwing his arms out and releasing the Da Vinci page which fluttered in the air and came to rest in a nearby flowerbed. Lindsey made a dash for the page and grabbed it, inadvertently uprooting a hand full of begonias at the same time. He retreated across the piazza shedding the flowerheads to left and right as he went. Louisa, unsure what to make of the sudden appearance of one of her companions, turned her attention to the inspector.

"Are you all right?"

"Yes, just bruised."

"There's blood on your forehead."

"It's nothing. The paper, where is it?"

"Gone. Lindsey's got it."

"Norov."

"Pardon?"

"His name's Norov."

"What do you mean?"

This question remained unanswered as Utter, who had found his glasses, helped the inspector to his feet.

"Look, we need to talk. My place is nearby, there are some things I need to explain to you and perhaps you can be of some help."

CHAPTER 28

INSPECTOR GRIPPE LED HIS young companions through an iron gate that led off the street. Scent from a flowering climber around the gate filled the air. They crossed a courtyard where roses had been planted, their weedy stems supporting a few blighted leaves and blown rose heads of indeterminate colour. Somewhere above them a radio played a sickly sub-opera tune. Louisa looked up and saw a woman operating a pulley system between the blocks of flats. As she drew the line in the woman unpegged dried clothes folding them into a basket balanced on a windowsill. The sound of the courtyard door closing behind them as they climbed the concrete stairway to the Inspector's flat echoed loudly in the empty stairwell.

Louisa and Utter stood on a terraced area that looked out onto a tarmacked play area, and some school buildings beyond. A group of boys were passing a basketball between them and taking shots at a ring hanging lopsidedly from a metal fencepost. Their voices were loud in the silence of the afternoon. Inspector Grippe called from the kitchen.

"Coffee?"

Inspector Grippe spun the gun metal casing of his coffee pot and lifted the strainer from the lower part of the pot. He banged the rim on the edge of the kitchen basin, the compact remains of his morning coffee coming away in sections. He refilled it and reassembled the hexagonal pieces. He told Utter where to find the cups and something to eat. Louisa wandered into the interior of the flat. The windows were shuttered against the heat of the day so that the rooms were cool and darkened. Rugs covered the stone flooring and ornately carved chairs populated the living areas. Glass cabinets stretched the length of the room filled with Venetian glassware and rows of books. Louisa came to the end of the cabinet and was transfixed. Breathing through both hands she said:

"My God. Cynthia. What are you doing here?"

The cabinet contained a framed photograph she recognized from cosy evenings spent in Cynthia's living room. Everything was the same except that instead of Doug Digit, a young Cynthia was leaning against the bonnet of a 'Combi' van. She was wearing a long dress. Beads were braided into her hair and she had a cowhide satchel on her shoulder. Underneath the picture it said 'Mohave Desert, 1968'. Louisa tried to work out Cynthia's expression.

She wondered if she had tired of smiling and the picture had been taken as her smile faded and her face relaxed.

"You were lovely," Louisa ran a finger over the picture.

"Yes, she was."

Inspector Grippe opened the shutters in the living room and set three cups of coffee onto a glass table.

"You have some questions. I will do my best to answer them."

Louisa wanted to ask why he had a picture of Cynthia in his display cabinet but instead she said:

"Why did Lindsey want that bit of paper?"

"First things first. You may know him as a college tutor but he has another identity altogether."

"Go on," Utter said.

"How's your European history?"

Utter and Louisa looked blankly at the Inspector.

"OK. Lindsey belongs to a group. They are known as the Berezina Brotherhood."

More blank looks.

"The Berezina is a river in Russia. In November 1812 it was a very busy place. Napoleon was retreating from Moscow pursued by Tsar Alexander's army. The French arrived in Borisov on the Berezina only to be faced by part of the Russian army on the other side of the river. Napoleon managed to bluff the Russians into thinking that he was going to make the crossing at Borisov by leaving a division of soldiers there while taking the bulk of the army north to Studzienka. Pontooneers waded into the river, put down piles and constructed two pontoons for the army to cross."

"Interesting history lesson but what has this to do with Louisa's tutor."

"Bear with me, this is important. Napoleon outsmarted the Russian high command and his army made it across the river. The point of telling you all this is that the man on the ground – one General Chichagov – knew what Napoleon was up to and was shadowing him on the other side of the river until he was told to return to Borisov. By the time the Russian Field Marshalls knew what was really happening it was too late. The French had slipped through their hands. Of course, Napoleon was defeated in the end but Chichagov and the officers who had fought on the

Berezina formed themselves into a brotherhood sworn to defend true leadership and to establish Russian dominance in Europe. This seemed to be happening by 1814 when crowds cheered the Tsar all the way up the Champs Elysees but it didn't last. The Berezina Brotherhood is based on ideas about national destiny and a dread of occupation - something that started when the Mogul hordes swept across Russia God knows how many centuries ago. The Brotherhood has survived Stalinism and Perestroika, but whatever the regime they have always been power brokers. Their visibility in the Kremlin has depended on the leadership at the time; under Stalin they actively encouraged his expansionist policies, under Gorbachev they sank back into the woodwork. After the wall fell Russia seemed to be destined for obscurity; free enterprise, the Russian Mafia all added up to chaos. Now things are different. The US have been pulling the bear's tail and the new leadership are fighting back; of course it's just diplomatic posturing at the moment – a new cold war, if you will – but the hand of the Berezina Brotherhood has become, how shall I say, more noticeable. This oil business is the opportunity they have been waiting for.

"Meaning?" said Utter.

"Meaning that they can bring Europe to its knees. It's experimenting with Georgia at the moment and that seems to be working nicely, like it will for the other old satellite states. Russia never really let them go – and now they need to be brought back into line. The main pipe line supplies into Europe are already being restricted."

"We've noticed."

"You wait – this hasn't even begun to have a real affect yet. It's only inconvenient at the moment. Once they start selling wholesale to China and India, Europe will feel the pinch in all sorts of ways."

Louisa, who had been trying very hard to follow what the Inspector had been saying, finished her coffee and said:

"I'm lost. Lindsey's just one of my tutors - how can he be part of a 'brotherhood' – it all sounds a bit cranky. It sounds like boys' stuff, all secret society and dodgy handshakes."

"Far from it. You saw what he was prepared to do today. If I told you that when the Kremlin gave up communism several high ranking party members declared their membership of the Berezina Brotherhood. Even the President is thought to have Brotherhood sympathies.

" OK, I still don't get it but here's another question. Has this got anything to do with the Russian man I recognized in the street today.

"What Russian man?"

"I don't know his name but I saw him at my college the day Mum and me visited."

"Smirka. So, he is here already."

"What?"

"Colonel Smirka. What did he look like?"

Louisa showed Inspector Grippe her sketch.

"Yes, a good likeness. Where did you see him?"

"We were somewhere in the city and he pulled up in a black car. He seemed to be waiting for someone and then went off in a hurry when he saw us."

"Louisa, I can't let you go back to your Mother at the moment. I'll tell her you are safe but Lindsey is a dangerous man and you would be an easy target if you were with your Mum and the others."

"What about me?" said Utter.

"You must stay here too until this is finished. There are more important things at stake. I will explain your theft of a priceless artefact. A youthful prank that went wrong. Like your banners, the theft was part of a – postmodernist statement, if you will. When you become a famous artist you can tell your biographer all about it, but for the moment we will quietly drop the matter."

The Inspector touched Utter's arm and smiled:

"Well, I will leave you now."

CHAPTER 29

LINDSEY NORTH UNTIED THE straps on Lucia's shoulders and her dress fell to the floor. Placing one hand on the small of her back he drew her to him. She cupped her hands behind his neck and opened her mouth. Her tongue found his with a shock of pleasure that made Lucia press her mound into his stiffening groin. He lifted her onto the white expanse of the bed. Gliding his hands over her slim body, he bent to take one of her nipples in his teeth. Arching her stomach, she drew him to her. Sweat bubbled on his back as he entered her.

Later, searching for his cigarettes in his discarded trousers, Lindsey took out the Da Vinci page he had wrested from the policeman and laid it beside a similar looking piece of paper: the mirror writing was there and a sketch, this time of the helicopter's cone, and two letters – CA. He took both pages and moved them together until the letters made a word – TOSCA. Lindsey thought about the preparations he would have to make to complete his mission. He disliked firearms, partly because they were difficult to conceal and to get rid of and partly because they were so unimaginative. He preferred a more creative method of elimination- something involving poison maybe, or a small explosion. He had been a sleeper long enough and was glad to be on active service for the Brotherhood. He sat on the edge of the bed and put his fingers on the nape of Lucia's neck, her hair falling away in a loose bun. She had wound the bedsheet around her giving her the appearance of an ascending grace. He lit another cigarette and looked out onto the city roofs and thought about the last time he had been on active service. He had recruited a visiting Russian professor whose idea of clandestine was a good lunch at the Randolph Hotel. To begin with, Lindsey was unsure why they wanted to have a professor of palaeontology specializing in permafrost. When he read an article about climate change in the Guardian he began to understand. Melting permafrost in the wastes of Siberia would mean a dangerous release of methane gas; it would also mean that Russia would have access to untold billions of tonnes of crude oil. The professor had been easy. This mission was an altogether different matter. The Brotherhood was enjoying one of its periods of influence and the flow of classified information meant that members had to be loyal and reliable. On his last visit to the allotments Lindsey had learned that a high ranking member of the Brotherhood was about to be very unreliable. Sitting in his steel lined potting shed he had written down his encrypted instructions and translated the message – the name Colonel Dimitri Smirka had been spelt out followed by one word- ELIMINATE. Lindsey pulled on his shirt and recalled that he had met Colonel Smirka several times; once in a concrete bunker inside Chechnya with the sound of automatic fire uncomfortably close and once in an office off Red Square when the Colonel had treated him with great suspicion: he remembered the Colonel shouting questions at him: what was the foreigner doing amongst them? How long had he been a member of the Brotherhood? What service record did he have? Lindsey had not been troubled by this - his credentials were immaculate. His grandparents were White Russians and had left Russia in 1919 taking a route on foot that made Napoleon's retreat from Moscow look like an afternoon stroll. It had taken them three years to reach Western Europe. Grandfather Norov taught Political Science at the Sorbonne until the Second World War broke out when he accepted a chair at Oxford. Lindsey remembered his grandparents as old people in his family home in the Banbury Road speaking a language to each other that he always thought was beautiful.

"Lindsey, come back to bed. We have more fun."

Lucia curled her hand around his taut waist and felt along the crease between his upper thigh and the flat of his stomach. Lindsey glanced at his watch and turned towards his latest conquest.

Chapter 30

"HE'S GOING TO LET you off," Louisa said.

"It seems so," Utter replied.

"You don't sound very grateful."

"He's just using us."

"He's protecting us."

"Maybe."

"Utter what's wrong?"

"I know him."

"From when? How do you know him?"

"He's helped me before," Utter spoke as if each word were torn from his throat.

"I'm listening."

"When I was sixteen I ran away from home. Bad things happened there and my parents didn't want me anymore. I lived on the street for a while and then I joined a squat. It was a relief to start with. They left me alone. The others. But it was bad at night. I used to find a corner so that I could see everything, watch out for myself. I set up a candle and drew whatever I saw around me, it was a way to keep me awake. Sleeping was dangerous. I was frightened but had nowhere else to go. I was on the street and this man said he wouldn't give me any money but he would buy me a meal. I thought he was a paedo but I was too hungry to care. I showed him my sketches. We arranged to meet again and this time he said he had found somewhere else for me to be. I went with him but he never touched me. He took me to a big building where I showed my pictures to a woman. She said that they were good. She ran an atelier, a kind of art school"

"Where was this? asked Louisa.

"In Holland. Where I grew up." " This man, the Inspector, was the man who helped me. He used to come and see how I was getting on and then he stopped coming, I didn't see him anymore."

"This was a long time ago, right?"

"Seven years ago. When I finished I stayed on as an assistant, sold some of my work, managed to get by."

"Poor you," Louisa said.

"Yes, poor me. Boo hoo."

Louisa put out her hand but Utter got up and raced around the room whooping and stamping his feet:

"Here in Italy we like to eat pasta, sing arias and dress up. We put scarves around our throats if we feel a little cold coming on and we do what our Mamma tells us to. We like to be very close to each other, with lots of hugs and kisses."

Each of these descriptions was accompanied by a grotesque mime and an exaggerated Italian accent until Louisa fell about laughing.

"Let's see what we can find," Utter said and began to look in drawers and cupboards.

"I don't think we should do that," said Louisa.

"Oh, come on, live a little." Utter said.

Louisa thought that Utter had lived a little bit too much.

"Let's find out about the mystery man," he said.

They moved from room to room but nothing caught their attention. There was no indication that the Inspector had a family or was part of any kind of community. They talked about the kinds of things that might reveal a life beyond the day to day routines of work.

"Golf clubs."

"Trophies."

"Family snaps."

"Somebody else's shoes."

"An address book."

"Souvenirs."

They rummaged through drawers and looked into wardrobes but discovered nothing.

"Just this picture," Louisa said.

"Ah, the love of his life, lost long ago."

"There's no need to be so cynical. Actually, I know who this is."

"Who?"

"It's my housemother at college. She's here, with the others."

CHAPTER 31

PANDORA FULBRIGHT AWAITED THE return of her companions. They had set off to find Louisa some hours before and she was now becoming a little worried, imagining that some accident had befallen them. Coincidentally, this worry was not altogether unfounded: unbeknown to her cyclists in the city were being mugged by loitering car drivers who, in the absence of fuel and being unable to pursue their daily business, were attacking cyclists and making off with their machines.

When the search party had gathered on the Via Sebastian it was decided that someone needed to stay behind in case the police found Louisa before they did. Pandora had willingly agreed to fulfill this role, sensing that the pursuit might not be good for her nerves. A small party of well wishers from the Hotel staff had gathered around the DeLouche riders; beautifully wrapped provisions were pressed upon them and hands warmly shaken – 'Buona fortuna, buona fortuna'. There was something epic about the event as if Ulysses were about to set off for the Trojan wars. Pandora was particularly struck by Steve's bearing as he sat astride his bike with his arms folded and it took her only a small leap of imagination to style herself as Penelope weeping with Telemachus at her side. She made sure that he was aware of her presence by squeezing his arm and wishing him a personal 'buona fortuna'. He had smiled down at her and made some remark about needing it and needles in haystacks.

Standing in the shade of the loggia, a place that had become their command post, Pandora looked towards the Duomo and remembered that she had not written one of her postcards that day. She reached into her handbag and counted the remaining three cards. Her neighbour having stacked the other seven neatly on the hall table at home might have wondered at these strange messages to the dead. Pandora had surprised herself by telling Steve Durrant about her mother. After all, he was the last person to confide in. She had always thought of him as bluff and insensitive and she knew that he made disparaging remarks about her behind her back. She suspected that her nickname – the birdwoman of DeLouche – had originated with him. But then there had been that moment in Montepuliano when another side to Steve had been revealed and suddenly she had found herself telling this man her innermost secrets. Talking about her mother's death had been a relief. She wondered if she had reached another stage in her grief – this process was well documented in the kind of women's magazines that Pandora flicked through between marking essays. By telling Steve about that awful day when she came home she had perhaps shed the power it had over her – a power that had made her write postcards to someone who was no longer alive. Was this what they called 'closure'? She felt no less bereft, no less lonely, but she could do without the postcards now, could begin to come away from the bleakness she had felt since that day. She felt that in some obscure way Steve was part of this redemption. She held the cards over the edge of the loggia wall and let them fall to the pavement below.

CHAPTER 32

"Beer?"

"Pope, Catholic."

The familiar shorthand being complete Duncan indicated 'Due Peroni' to the waiter who hovered at his shoulder.

"Quite a morning."

The two men shifted uneasily in their chairs

"Talk about saddle-sore," said Duncan.

"And the rest. I've got bruises all over me. Hit by flying bits of rock, barged by angry prelates or whoever they were, generally shaken up – and all for nothing. The little bugger got away from us."

"Yes, Mrs B is not happy. I wouldn't like to be Louisa when she catches up with her."

"No. But at least the girl didn't look as if she'd been kidnapped. Where did they get a tandem from! Actually, she looked fine, grinning from ear to ear. We must have looked pretty stupid puffing after her like that," said Steve.

"The younger generation sticking two fingers at us. I envy them really."

"Now then no midlife crisis stuff please, we've enough to cope with without you getting all maudlin. Anyway, she looked all right, we've just got to keep Daphne on track until the daughter gets fed up with her Elvis Costello lookalike and decides to come back."

"Yes, the bloke looked harmless enough, I had visions of her being taken off my some aging lothario with patent leather shoes and a gold chain round his neck," said Duncan.

"Shouting out where we're staying was a good idea. At least the parent's here, there won't be a complaint about losing a child."

"Funny you should say that. I saw another parent this morning."

"A yummy Mummy staying at her villa with the children while hubby pursues another city bonus?"

"Tut,tut, bitter, bitter. No, it was Ivan Smirka's father. You know, Colonel Smirka," said Duncan.

"Ah, yes, with the drop dead gorgeous 'secretary'."

"He wasn't with his secretary when I saw him today."

They drank their beer in silence.

"I noticed that the birdwoman was paying particular attention to you when we left this morning," said Duncan.

"I thought you disapproved." Steve paused and then said: "I'm not very proud of that one, if we could just drop it. Pandora and I … things have changed."

"Well, I'm very grateful. Perhaps she'll pay less attention to me."

"Don't get ideas. I'm too much of an old bachelor to be interested."

"Not so old, Steve, but the clock is ticking for you."

"Thank you for pointing it out but I don't think it's any of your business."

"Probably not but we've known each other long enough for me to take a few liberties."

"I'm sorry. You're right. I'm a bit nervous, that's all. Lived how I've liked, gone where I've wanted to go, done what I've wanted to do, not done what I've not wanted to do. It's been good, but …"

"Nuff said."

"We, Pandora and me, we… She's all right."

"Good."

"Did you notice those postcards on the pavement when we got back? I wondered if they might be Pandora's."

"Why would she throw her postcards away?"

"Her Mother's dead, you know. Died before we left for Italy."

"Well I never. Extraordinary."

Darling D

*Poor you – silly girl worrying her Mum like that. At least I
know where Sarah is, in body anyway. She e mailed Simon,
did he say? Full of complaints about us, me in particular
– you seem to have avoided most of the criticism. Very unfair! Apparently I'm a control freak and spoil everything.
Something about taking Simon away from her. I think our
Simon gave me a sanitised version to protect me from the
more florid moans. How lovely that Steve and Pandora have
found each other – I'm only surprised it took them so long.
We must encourage them.*

Come home soon. Love Claire xxxxx

CHAPTER 33

INSPECTOR GIUSEPPE GRIPPE STOOD before the assembled DeLouche cycling party and prepared to take them into his confidence.

"Ladies and gentlemen, I need to ask for your help."

He paused and looked at each member of the party, glancing only briefly at Cynthia Digit.

"The day has been very eventful. Some of you have put yourself at great personal risk in the service of Mrs Bowler and her daughter. Alas, partly in vain. You have established that she is still in the city and that she is alive and well.

Mrs Bowler snorted at this assertion and turned away from the Inspector.

"And well," he repeated.

"I can now reveal that I have spoken to Louisa today and can confirm that she is in good health."

"What, what are you saying?" Daphne Bowler exploded in disbelief.

"Mrs Bowler, calm yourself. Louisa wishes to thank you all for your concern and apologizes for any anxiety she may have caused."

"Anxiety! She's ruined the holiday and lost me any commercial credibility I might have had."

"Nonsense, Daphne. All of this has been out of your control, and we are only concerned that Louisa comes back to us safely," Duncan said.

"She is with a young friend and is in good hands," the Inspector continued.

"Take me to her immediately, Inspector."

"I'm afraid that won't be possible. You see, while she is with me she is safe. She would be too … exposed … without my protection."

Duncan rose to his feet.

"This hasn't got anything to do with Lindsey North, has it?"

The thought of the lascivious Lindsey pawing at the innocent Louisa made Duncan feel very uncomfortable and he was not reassured by the Inspector's reply.

"You will know that Lindsey North declined to come with you when you left San Verino. In fact, he is in the city and has been for some time now."

"Oh my God. He's got Louisa. This is a nightmare. What's he done to her, where is she?" said Daphne rising from her chair.

The inspector waited for the mood to settle. As an officer of the law conveying bad news he was quite used to people focusing on the part of what he said that confirmed their worst fears.

"Mrs Bowler, your daughter has not been harmed by Lindsey North or anyone else. I need you all to listen very carefully. I am not at liberty to explain the whole situation at the moment, suffice it to say that unless I have your cooperation a delicate situation will be made much worse, possibly catastrophic."

"Inspector, this is all very opaque. What exactly do you want us to do?"

"Nothing."

"Nothing. That's going to be very hard."

"Nevertheless, you must do nothing. This will all become clear in a very short time and Louisa will be back amongst you."

"No, I cannot tolerate this, I insist that you take me to Louisa now."

Cynthia Digit's belief in her husband's sincerity had, understandably, been shaken. Nevertheless, she knew more about him than anyone else in the group and so now she summoned up her old loyalty to him.

"Daphne, this man needs our agreement. He clearly knows things we don't. We need to trust him."

Cynthia led Daphne Bowler back to her chair and sat her down. Suddenly, the wind seemed to have gone out of her sails. Her command of the situation deserted her and she fell into an unaccustomed acquiescence.

CHAPTER 34

LINDSEY WATCHED THE LITTLE figure turn on the dome of the San Salute church. When the miniature sail caught the breeze it flashed gold in the late afternoon sun. Across the street the entrance to the church was busy with the traffic of those attending the evening service. He waited. A car lucky enough to have found some petrol passed in the street, the sight being unusual enough to make heads turn. Checking his watch, he moved into a position where he could observe the church door unseen either by those entering or leaving the building. He looked up at the little figure again. The wind had shifted to the East and all he could see now were the two little buttocks of the statue as the wind moved the sail around. Looking back at the church entrance he saw Inspector Grippe pushing open the glass inner door and enter the church. He recognized the Inspector from their tussle earlier that day and from the file information which told him that he was a CIA operative. After some minutes he saw Colonel Smirka moving diagonally across the wide church steps. The Russian paused at the top of steps and looked around before he, too, disappeared through the glass door.

Lindsey stood for a moment in the church interior until his eyes were accustomed to the gloom. A metal framework supported rows of little cylinders into which candles had been lodged, light flickering from their thin stems. Worshippers made the sign of the cross, selected a candle from a tin box and held the wick over one of the lit candles before adding it to the others. This act of devotion completed, they moved forward into the body of the church. Five wheelchairs had been parked beside the main aisle pews, their occupants still and concentrated. Beside each of them was a nun in a blue and white habit, their faces obscured by extravagantly winged headdresses. Ahead of him at the altar Lindsey saw the priest dressed in white vestments. A microphone was placed on the altar and the priest lent towards it as he intoned the sanctus, his words amplified to tinny resonance. Acolytes stood at his side and passed the paraphernalia of devotion to him. The priest held a communion chalice above his head and, having taken the blood and body of Christ, held his hands open in a gesture of welcome and as a signal that those wishing to receive communion should come forward. Lindsey scanned the church to locate the American and Smirka. He saw Smirka first, his head bent in prayer, surrounded by other worshippers. This powerful figure known in the Brotherhood for his ability to intimidate, seemed changed in his posture of obeisance. Lindsey was surprised to see that this pillar of the Brotherhood was not only the servant of the Russian state but also of the Holy Roman church.

Lindsey looked to his left and along the side aisle. The Virgin Mary recently paraded in the streets was the first of a series of statues stretching the length of the wall. A bedraggled bouquet of flowers surrounded the Virgin's feet. Lindsey could not see the American anywhere. Halfway up the side aisle was a confessional. The dark wood box looked as if it had just been dumped in the aisle to keep it out of the way. He could see the legs of the penitent beneath the 'saloon' door of the confessional and, on the other side, the priest's trainers visible under his cassock. Lindsey moved up the aisle being careful to stay just behind the kneeling Smirka. Then he saw the American. He was in the opposite side aisle with his back to him studying a canvas depicting the passion of Christ. Beside him was a group of tourists, commentary receivers pressed to their ears. This was his opportunity. He waited until the last of the communicants had filed out of the pew behind Smirka and then moved swiftly to sit behind him. He waited to see if Colonel Smirka would take communion, after all he seemed to be taking part in the rest of the service. He did not move; his head was bowed and he was kneeling on the prayer rail running along the back of the pew in front of him. For a moment Lindsey wondered if the American had got there first. He glanced to his side but the little group around the painting had dispersed and the American was nowhere to be seen.

"Must you disturb me now?"

"I have come to ask you to change your mind."

"It is too late."

"You know what I must do."

"I know. But not here."

"No, not here."

Lindsey watched the back of Colonel Smirka's head as if it would show some sign of weakness, of retraction, of returning to the fold. The Colonel was a man of influence, would be familiar with decisions being made at the highest level, was known as a Berezinist to whom the powerful listened. Once he was in the hands of the West who could say where it would all end. The Americans were busy installing their listening posts in the old satellite states, next they would be putting in their missile silos. It was intolerable.

And now this man was about to give them the justification they needed.

"Why are you doing this?" Lindsey asked.

"I am tired."

"Tired?"

"Of these games."

"This is not a game. Have you forgotten your pledge as a Berezinist? You are important. You have kept the faith for so long, have sacrificed so much – all those years in Chechnya, the dangers. This is a betrayal. We have a chance to make Russia great again and you … I don't understand it. "

"We have all been deluded. Hanging on to a dream that our great-grandfathers spun out of a land devastated by war and bankrupted by inequality and complacency. We took our revenge in 1945, what we did in Berlin and the rest of Germany was enough. Berezinists – pah. Sentimentalists all of you, we have a place in the new politics but our idealism is dangerous. It is the politics of madness. Holding Europe to ransom with our oil like gangsters! It must be exposed."

Lindsey looked around the church impatiently, the Colonel's words bouncing off the carapace of his convictions.

"The American – is he here to take you?" said Lindsey.

"Yes."

"When?"

"Do you think I will make it that easy for you?"

The priest said the peace and switched off the microphone. The choir boys went behind the altar and reappeared carrying trestle tables from behind the altar. The tables would be put against the church door and taken out into the street the next day for the neighbourhood Sagra. Already, in houses and apartments families were baking bread and decanting wine and preparing the home grown produce. Colonel Smirka left the church and was lost in the narrow streets that weaved away from it.

Chapter 35

Duncan wandered through the San Salute 'sagra' pleased to be away from the neurotic atmosphere of the Palazzo Bignole. He had taken the Inspector at his word and decided that doing nothing was the best course of action. If the abortive chase had not been enough to convince him of this modus operandi then the ominous hints of the Inspector had driven the point home. He was reminded of the Chinese curse –'May you live in interesting times'. Well, he thought, things had got far too interesting of late and this excursion into normality was just what was needed. Bright red and green awnings had been erected above the trestle tables from the church and improvised fans kept the flies away from the dolce breads. Duncan thought it time to try out his Italian. Stopping by a stall groaning with breads he pointed at one of them and said:

"Cos'e questo?"

"Prego?"

"That – what is it?"

"Ah, questa. Questa e' pasta di mandorle."

"Une tranche, a bit."

Duncan made a cutting gesture with his hand. The vendor, realising that he was in the presence of a foreigner, smiled encour-
agingly at him and forgave his customer for thinking he was in
France.

"Eccola. Una euro, per favor."

Duncan bit into the bread and made yumyum noises.

"Ti piace," said the stall holder.

"I should coco."

He reached a sticky hand over the table, carried away by the sus-
tained communication he had managed with his fellow European.
The next table was occupied with a single bread elaborately woven
into the shapes of the city emblems. His view of this masterpiece
of doughmanship was obscured by two nuns who had been pushing wheelchairs but had abandoned them to gaze at the work-
manship of the panne cita. The nuns wore starched headgears
covering the side of their faces in a Catholic version of the burkah.
He became aware that his name was being called and thought that
he was in the grip of some divine revelation brought on by his
proximity to the nuns. His attention was caught by arms waving
at him from the loggia of the Palazzo Bignole. Waving back at
Cynthia he stayed where he was and waited for her to catch up
with him. Finishing off his Mandorle he invested in a Pasta Frolla,
managing to finish it before Cynthia reached him.

"Thanks for waiting, Duncan. Couldn't stand being the supportive
type anymore."

"Here try a…" Duncan peered at a label,passed over some loose
change to a boy who was manning the family stall and handed
Cynthia a Pasta Genovese.

"By the time we get to the end of this street I will have laid the foundations for a long afternoon sleep."

"And a heart attack," Cynthia said.

"Spoilsport. We're on holiday."

"You wouldn't think so back there. Mrs B looking like thunder and refusing to speak and Steve and Pandora behaving very oddly indeed. What's going on there?"

"I think they're getting to know each other, if you see what I mean."

"Well they're going about it in a very odd way. Long silences broken by synchronized blurting that leads to more silence. Why don't they just get on with it."

"Perhaps they don't know what to do," Duncan said.

Cynthia bought two grappa and a large slice of panne olio.

"Duncan, I need to talk to you, to tell you something."

She gave one of the glasses to Duncan and broke the Panne in half.

"Cynthia, if you're about to declare your undying love for me, you must stop."

He bit into the panne olio and downed the Grappa.

"On second thoughts, another one of those and I'm yours."

They wondered along the line of tables, Cynthia engaging the stallholders in passable Italian. Reaching the end of the street, they sat on the steps of the San Salute.

"Duncan, Doug's here."

Duncan blinked. Cynthia gave him a moment and then continued.

"I know. He was dead. I mean, I thought he was dead but he isn't. I met him today. So did you."

"Cynthia, what are you talking about? Your husband died in San Francisco thirty years ago"

"He's Inspector Grippe."

"What?"

"I mean he's become Inspector Grippe."

Duncan considered saying something about losing her grip but thought that this was probably not the time for cheap jokes.

"Cynthia, please explain."

"He came up to see about Louisa. Of course I recognized him straight away. He was ...heavier and he'd lost a lot of hair. We'd all had a lot to lose then."

Cynthia laughed and Duncan thought about the picture in Cynthia's room.

"But the same eyes, I think it was his eyes I fell in love with first of all. He was Paul Newman and Robert Redford all rolled into one when you looked at his eyes. Anyway, when I saw him I fainted."

"I'm not surprised. But he told you, explained."

"Yes. His death had been faked and the funeral."

Cynthia drew in her breath and her body shook. Duncan waited.

"He was a CIA agent monitoring anti-war activists. He was about to be exposed so they faked his death and moved him on."

"And you had no idea."

"Not the faintest. Funny isn't it? I was so innocent, I believed in him absolutely. We were so in love, I thought. But he had other ... loyalties."

"And then?"

"Vietnam, working with the South Vietnamese. He had ... a good war ...a distinguished service record. Then other hot spots-Afghanistan, Iran. He never got in touch. He never tried. It was as if I had never existed. There's so much that hurt but that ..."

"And now he's just an Italian copper."

"No. He's still working for the CIA when he's needed. This is where your Russian comes in, I think."

"In what way?"

"I think Doug's been assigned to receive him."

"Receive him?"

"You know, take him. Colonel Smirka is about to defect and Doug's his first contact.""

"Defect."

"Do stop repeating what I say."

"Sorry, Cynthia but all this takes a bit of getting used to. I didn't think people needed to defect anymore."

"If they're important enough they do."

"Did Doug tell you all this?"

"Not directly."

Cynthia paused to allow Duncan to absorb this. She did not tell him about Lindsey getting out of the Inspector's car. She would tell him later.

"There's another bit to the story."

"Go on."

"Doug and I had a baby. Or rather I had the baby – after his death."

"Are you still in touch?"

"No. I gave him away."

"In America?"

"In Bucharest. After the accident and the funeral and everything I discovered that I was pregnant. I didn't know what to do with myself. I had my green card so I stayed. I'd got some credits from Berkeley and I decided to finish my degree."

"In?"

"Political Science. We'd been very active. We were Marxists. Well, I was a Marxist. There was a study visit to Romania so I went. That's where I had the baby."

"But didn't you want to keep it?"

"No. Anyway, being a single mother was difficult in those days – even in the early 70's."

"I left him in the hospital."

"Him?"

"I didn't name him."

Cynthia took another deep breath and looked around at the young people sitting on the church steps.

"And, yes, of course, I have regrets. But I was alone. I didn't think it would matter so much. Out of sight, out of mind. Plenty to get on with – I had my degree to finish, maybe a masters, getting a career."

"Does Doug know?"

"He said he did – how he knew beats me."

"Maybe he was keeping in touch."

"How? Spying on me? That's not what I call keeping in touch."

"Perhaps he knows where your son is."

"I don't want to know. It's hard enough working out what to do with Doug."

"Has he asked to come back."

"No. Not yet."

White vans wove along the Via Sebastian and began to pack away the 'sagra'. Trestle tables were folded and borne aloft into the church. Vendors peered into their leather aprons and counted the day's takings while small boys called to upper windows to be let in, their voices rasping and raucous in a peculiarly Italian way. Duncan looked along the street and saw Daphne pacing on the loggia of their hotel.

"Come on, Cynth. Time to go back and do nothing again."

Darling D

What news! How is Cynthia coping? What a shock. Is he married? What's he been doing all this time! I bet you haven't asked about it — typical male! I want all the low-down — shall I write a list of questions? It's brilliant news, or is it ? How does she feel? And what's this about Lindsey the lech? Write soon.

CHAPTER 36

UTTER GRIPPED A LENGTH of gaffa tape in his teeth and ripped it away from the spool. He smoothed the tape along one side of a black silk sheet and then instructed Louisa to fix the sheet to the top of the window. When this was done he took another length of tape and secured the hanging sheet to the side of the window frame. Utter repeated this procedure on the other side of the window.

"We need a section to go above and below so that we make a space in the middle."

Louisa selected some pillowcases from a chest in the hallway where they had discovered the bed linen was kept and brought them into the kitchen. She laid them on the table and smoothed out the creases, applying the gaffa tape to one side and handed one end to Utter. They taped the pillowcases to the top of the window frame. Fixing the other pillowcases to the lower section proved more difficult but they ran a length of string across the front of the window and secured either end. They draped the pillowcase over the string. Utter lifted a piece of cardboard onto the table and began to cut it to the size of the space left at the centre of the black material. When he had completed this he cut a square out of the cardboard so that it became a frame.

"Hold this on the space."

The kitchen was now in darkness except for a square of light that broke over the cupboards at the back of the room. Utter pushed his glasses onto the bridge of his nose and peered through the window. He had placed a heavily carved chair on the kitchen terrace outside the new 'window'. Louisa moved the chair until he was satisfied that it was in the correct position. Utter then made a tripod out of three broom handles tying them together at the top with tea towels.

"OK, now you must wait."

Utter ushered Louisa out of the room and closed the door. He cut another strip of cardboard and made a lip along the top of the frame. Pinning a sheet of white paper to a thin chopping board he secured it next to the window. Returning to the tripod he jammed the metal legs of a shaving mirror into the soft material that held it together. Moving the mirror carefully up and down and sideways, glancing at the sheet of paper each time, he found the correct angle. He put one of the kitchen chairs next to the window and opened Louisa's Pocahontas pencil case. He placed it on the table so that she could reach it from the chair. Finally, he taped the last of the silk sheets to the top of the door frame so that no light could enter.

When he left the room he found Louisa pacing around the hallway.

"Almost time. I must get ready."

He told her to sit down and close her eyes. He went out onto the terrace and put on a scarlet coloured 'pillbox' hat and threw a heavily embroidered drape over his shoulders so that only his head was visible. He arranged himself on the chair.

"OK, open your eyes now."

Louisa blinked and covered her mouth in delight and surprise. Sitting in the chair Utter had placed for her she let out a little scream. On the sheet of paper next to the window was an upside down image of Utter.

"You look very noble. I wonder where your palace is, and how many servants you have."

The image was very sharp and, for reasons to do with light and refraction, was not reversed. Louisa picked out her favourite 2B pencil and began to draw.

...

The idea of making a mirror-lens for Louisa came to Utter when he looked at her sketch book. Her drawings were very good. They recorded the events of her holiday in quick sketches annotated with comments. In the latter sketches he had recognized himself – his spiky figure next to some of his exhibits; sitting on the front of a tandem his hair swept back to suggest great speed; at the contessa's feast, his presence reduced to a pair of black rimmed glasses shown on the top of a dish of steaming pasta. Louisa's drawings were a mass of marks that worked towards the desired image. He had read somewhere about Camera Obscurae and Vermeer's use of optics and how an artist had noticed the difference between continuous lines in a drawing and lines that indicated a groping towards shape and substance and had explained it by the difference between artists who had used optical devices and those who had not. He had thought about making a simple camera obscura – the strangeness of producing an image by merely confining light to a pin prick had appealed to him but then he had considered

the difficulties of light sensitivity relative to the size of the hole
and was not sure if he could make the thing 'work'. He decided
that making a mirror-lens would be more fun and would give
Louisa more scope.

Louisa had asked no questions when he had told her to hunt the
flat for the materials needed to build the dark-room and set up
the mirror-lens but had gone about her task with a childlike trust
in her friend. She had no idea what he was up to but felt that, on
previous evidence, there would be some treat at the end, some
bit of magic that would delight and entertain her. Louisa was not
used to this sort of attention, especially from boys. She realized
Utter's interest in her was not physical and this had been both a
relief and a disappointment. On their first night in the flat they
had sat in the kitchen and drunk a bottle of wine and Utter had
spoken about what he called the art industry fascists and Louisa
had listened to him and become a little drunk and had played
with his bare feet beneath the table but he had not seemed to
notice and had gone on talking until she pulled her feet away
from his and got up and said good night and left her. She had
not known what to make of the situation and had tried not to
feel rejected. Louisa did not consider the possibility that Utter
would not have responded to any girl who had played with his
toes beneath the table. She reasoned that she and Utter had been
thrown together by chance and forced into each other's company.
Had it been otherwise she was sure that he would have moved
on by now, bored of her company, bored of her not knowing
anything, bored of her dazed blankness in the face of the world.
But Utter seemed not to mind that she didn't know anything; that
she made mistakes and got her words mixed up and was 'as daft as
a brush' as her mother was fond of saying and that she had come
to believe. She had never had a boyfriend, the cool kids at school
had seen to that. She recalled that each morning when she left for
school there was some reminder of her helplessness: she had lost

something or she was late or had forgotten to do something – the accretions of failure confirming a sense of herself that said she was hardly worth taking notice of at all. And then the battleground of school where lesson-times were spent trying to be as invisible as possible and break-times where those around her, the cool kids, made sure she was. And in the end she did not need these others to tell her of her inadequacies because she carried them around with her – jailers who foiled every attempt at escape. But in all of this education about herself there had been something else – a still, small voice that called to her every time she picked up a pencil and made marks. And this voice said that there was another Louisa who could be at peace and not feel threatened or put down. It was this balm to her hurt mind that filled her now as she leaned to the white paper on the wall and began.

She started at the edge of Utter's chin and followed the line down to his mouth and then the tip of his nose and onto the indentation that ended with his eye brow. When she had finished the outline of his face she drew his hat in one continuous mark. She made measurements with her thumb and the flat edge of her pencil and then marked the paper accordingly. She saw that the pattern on the drape was repeated and so she made a detailed drawing of one part of it and then quickly noted the crease lines. Taking the board off the wall to work on her drawing Utter's image was replaced by her own. At first she could not work out how this had happened – after all, she should have been looking at the same image only darkened by the removal of the white paper. Instead what she saw was an image of herself, her features reduced by the dark background. At the edges of her image that floated in the air, tiny pinpricks of light shone through where the material was worn. Looking for an explanation for this phenomenon she saw that there was a make up mirror balanced on a shelf above the cooker. Somehow, in moving, Louisa had positioned herself to allow the two mirrors to alter the direction of the light and so produce another image.

"Isn't this a bit like cheating?" said Louisa.

"It's what they all did, the masters."

Louisa sat by the window and worked on the outline of her drawing. She worked quickly, replacing pencils and choosing other ones from her pencil case with accustomed actions, sometimes keeping a pencil between her lips to save time. The creases of Utter's 'gown' were heavily etched into the paper, at the edges of the drawing the geometric shapes in the material seemed to take a slightly different direction, the result of the lens position producing a distortion that Louisa then corrected by eye on the paper.

When she had finished the drawing she showed Utter who said how good a draughtswoman she was and Louisa had thanked him for making it all possible and for giving her such a lovely surprise.

"Perhaps we should take all of this away before the Inspector returns."

Utter was peeling the gaffa tape away when Louisa told him to stop.

"Look. Oh my God."

Louisa reversed the white chopping board and held it up in its original position. She beckoned to Utter not to stand in front of the window. The blurred image of Lindsey North crossed the wall and was illuminated by the whiteness of the chopping board. He stopped in direct line with the window and his image became very clear. Holding a small tube in his hand he looked directly at the kitchen terrace. Louisa had the uncomfortable feeling that he was also looking straight at them. His image swam into a blur and disappeared.

Darling D

*I have now discovered why Sarah's paramour is called Fist.
It's not pleasant. Sarah arrived home with a nasty bruise on
her arm. I was half way to the front door with Simon's laundry bag and getting ready to bar his entry to the house when
Sarah told me to stop jumping to conclusions. Apparently he
had intervened in a fight and saved Sarah from anything
worse than a few knocks. It was all a case of mistaken identity
in the emo sub culture. A group of girls had mistaken Sarah
for some other person who had transgressed the emo code of
conduct in some way. Simon had been vigorous in Sarah's
defence putting aside normal prohibitions about hitting girls
and weighed in. I don't remember our generation doing this
sort of thing. Perhaps we were just protected. Anyway, Sarah
is OK so don't worry. The dishwasher has packed up and I've
had to get a new one.*

Love Claire xxx

CHAPTER 37

DUNCAN WAS NOT AN opera buff but he found himself tapping his feet as the peasant chorus belted out a tune he recognised from Classic FM. The huge open-air auditorium in which he sat with the remaining members of the DeLouche party was packed with people. In front of them the city ramparts that formed the back wall of the stage rose impressively. Gantries banked with stage lights were arranged at the side of the stage and shone on three groups of performers. Soldiers and wagons, complete with four horses, were opposite a group of peasants dressed in rags and smeared with dirt. Centrestage was taken by a performer in a blue and white military uniform waving a fan, his barrel chest swelling as he delivered his part of a duet. Next to him stood the leading lady who was crying loudly. Cannon fire was heard off stage. Duncan could not understand a word they were saying and had not read the programme notes, however, it was clear that things had reached an emotional stage. The actors were gesturing wildly at each other and the wind section in the orchestra pit was reaching a crescendo; church bells pealed over the surging sound of trumpets. When the duet finished the actors bowed their heads and the Te Deum in the background faded away. The audience appeared to have been stunned into silence for a moment and then they erupted into applause and shouts of 'Bravo, Bravo.'

"Cracking. Shame Daphne isn't here she'd 've liked it," Steve said.

"Not in her present state," said Duncan.

"No, probably right. Pan and me are off to the bar."

Duncan noticed none of the awkwardness reported by Cynthia. In fact, they looked very happy in each other's company. He thought he saw Steve take Pandora's hand as they disappeared into the crowd but couldn't be sure. The evening at the opera was a central feature of the 'Two Wheels Good, Italy' package. The DeLouche party had set off from the Palazzo Bignole dressed in their best clothes. Linen suits and dresses had lain at the bottom of their cases for this very occasion. When they reached the Opera House most of the creases had fallen out in the warm evening air and they looked quite presentable, although unmistakably English. They walked through the streets in company with the local opera goers and felt, despite their best efforts, underdressed. Women in high heels and expensive dresses tottered beside their escorts. The men draped pastel coloured jackets over their shoulders allowing the brilliant whiteness of their shirts to be seen to the best advantage. In the absence of Daphne, Duncan had assumed the role of party leader. He had listened to the excited chatter of his three remaining companions and thought how much Claire would have enjoyed this evening and how much it was wasted on him. In many ways she had been the one who had given him his cultural education. She took him to films that she said were 'important' and fed him a diet of Booker prize-winners that would enable him to contribute to conversations at dinner parties. He had even joined her book group for a while but found the competitive atmosphere uncomfortable. He remembered a particular evening when the novel under inspection had involved marital breakdown and this had led to an embarrassing scene between a husband and wife which ended in the wife bursting into tears and the husband storming out of the room. After that Duncan thought that there were dangers lurking in the apparently benign groups of friends who gathered together in the name of literary appreciation. Other parts of his education had involved Opera. Claire had thought that he was ready to climb the slopes of high art and so seats had been booked for two operas by Puccini, these being judged by Claire as 'manageable'. The performances were midweek and took place an hour's drive away. By the time the second act had started the warmth and the darkness and the end of the working day combined to send Duncan to sleep and Claire to realise that opera had been an expensive failure.

"What a wonderful evening. Look, the stars are all out, it's a warm evening and here we are listening to an Italian opera in Italy surrounded by Italians."

Cynthia was looking through her opera glasses.

"I say, things seem to have moved on – Steve's put his arm around Pandora."

Duncan was not listening. His attention was fixed on the figure of Colonel Smirka who was sitting at one end of the front row. Inspector Grippe was sitting next to him. They leaned towards each other and Colonel Smirka was nodding in agreement with something the Inspector was saying.

Steve returned from the bar with two glasses of white wine.

"That was amazing. Like queuing up with a line of mafia bosses - some of them still had their dark glasses on. And their women – talk about bling."

"Yes, I felt very plain by comparison."

"Nonsense, Pan. Most of them were mutton dressed up as lamb. You look very nice."

The audience took their seats and the stage lights brightened. The blue and white uniform appeared and looked around melodramatically. Duncan wondered if this was intentional, a convention familiar to opera lovers, or merely a case of overacting. In fact, now that he had read the programme notes, he decided that this was a very silly story with practically no substance. He was tempted to lump opera together with most of Shakespeare's plays which he felt suffered from the same lack of credibility. When he expressed these opinions at social gatherings he was either seen as exposing the naked emperor, or condemned as a philistine. Either way, Claire would know he was only teasing. He suddenly felt very bereft without her. The music gathered momentum: drums rolled, and the brass section set up a repeated refrain accompanied by the intermittent sound of more cannon fire. Smoke drifted across the stage, suddenly busy with the entire cast: soldiers and peasants mingled with each other and turned to the audience and began a choric outburst of singing. The woman sitting next to Duncan put her hands together and said 'Bella, bella' as the leading lady swept onto the stage, her vermillion coloured dress ballooning and swaying as she took her place. The orchestra wove the repeated phrasing of the first act like an echo into the new scene and the string section came in with soaring unison. Soldiers marched onto the stage and lined up facing a character who tore his shirt theatrically and bared his chest to what was now a firing squad. The soldiers pointed their rifles and the hapless character fell to the floor. Duncan was suddenly aware that Colonel Smirka and Inspector Grippe had left their seats. As he turned to walk up the aisle Colonel Smirka's right hand moved to his neck, as if he had been bitten by a mosquito. After a moment he seemed to stagger and Inspector Grippe helped him to the back of the seating. In the same instant that Colonel Smirka was struck Duncan saw Lindsey North on his feet and lowering his hands to his side. Inspector Grippe seemed to glance at him but then continued to support the faltering Colonel. Lindsey moved up a parallel aisle and, jostling one of the front-of-house ushers, pushed open a fire exit and was gone.

"My God, did you see that?"

Cynthia had her opera glasses trained on the Diva.

"It's all right, Duncan, he hasn't really been shot."

Inspector Grippe now looked directly at Duncan and moved his index finger from side to side. He must have known where they were all sitting and now pre-empted any action they might be about to take. Duncan, who had half raised himself out of his seat, sat back down again.

"It's Smirka: something's just happened to him."

Cynthia lowered her opera glasses and turned to Duncan.

"Is this a clairvoyant moment or has the opera got to your imagination?"

"No, I'm serious. Grippe or Digit or whatever his name is has just left with him, he seemed to be ill. I saw Lindsey. You don't think …"

"Duncan, you're the only one left who is not suffering from trauma or a personality change! Please pull yourself together!"

Cynthia pointed at the stage.

"I think this is the climax."

The leading lady swept onto the stage and fell at the side of the stricken body and removed a blood soaked cloth. Duncan's attention was drawn back to the stage by the hysterical outburst following this action. The orchestra underlined this intense moment by piercing the night with waves of crashing sound. The violinists stabbed the air with their bows and the distraught female character disappeared over the back of the stage. There was uproar. Duncan had decided that continuing to do nothing was an impossibility. He was carried to his feet by the woman next to him who refused to let him out into the aisle until a full appreciation of the performance had been shown. By the time this was done and Duncan had struggled to the back of the seating, Inspector Grippe and the Colonel were nowhere to be seen.

The wailing sirens of the ambulance came to an abrupt halt and the crew set to work. The Colonel had managed to reach the exit but had collapsed on the pavement. Inspector Grippe had knelt by him and felt the skin at the side of his neck. His fingers came into contact with a pin like object sticking into his flesh. He drew it out being careful not to scratch his hand. Paramedics gave the prone figure of Colonel Smirka a brief medical assessment and lifted him onto a stretcher. An opera house manager stood by looking anxious. One of the ushers, thinking that the man had merely fainted, had fetched a glass of water. The ambulance doors were closed and the siren reactivated as it pulled onto the road. Inspector Grippe watched the tail lights of the ambulance as it headed for the city hospital. He sniffed the dart that Lindsey North had expertly lodged in the Colonel's neck and recognised the sickly smell of curare. Washington would not be happy and he would have some explaining to do if this Berezinist died before they had time to 'process' him. He sniffed the dart again: the curare would only paralyse him temporarily but before Colonel Smirka was taken away he noticed a dusting of powder around the dart puncture in his neck.

CHAPTER 38

Duncan Andrew and Inspector Grippe sat beside each other in a hospital corridor. The Inspector fiddled with his cigarette lighter and said:

"You were supposed to stay away from this."

"Inspector, Colonel Smirka's son is one of my students."

This statement struck neither of the men as an adequate explanation for his presence in the hospital. Duncan tried again.

"Look, what I saw brought me here. Lindsey North was responsible wasn't he?"

"Norov. Yes."

"I beg your pardon?"

"His name is Norov."

"Norov. Right."

This was all beginning to sound like a bad dream and Duncan was not sure whether he wanted anymore information.

"He's one of your tutors. I know. Has Cynthia told you who I am?"

"Yes. All I'm concerned about is reuniting Louisa with her mother so that we can all go home. Then you can carry on planting cameras in rocks and firing poison darts at each other without our getting in the way."

Duncan hoped that the CIA agent would not give him the line about doing the dirty work so that people like him could sleep safely in their beds.

"Mother and daughter will be reunited as soon as I've dealt with your Mr North."

Duncan did not ask what he meant by 'dealt with' but he feared the worst. Two nurses walked past them, the starch in their white uniforms making a swishing sound.

"Inspector, is Colonel Smirka going to die."

"I'm waiting for the medics to tell me that. "

Despite himself, Duncan asked more questions until Inspector Grippe told him what he had told Utter and Louisa. He spoke about the Berezinists and how they were in positions of power within the Kremlin hierarchy and that, as a prominent member of the brotherhood Colonel Smirka was well placed to know what was behind Russia's oil embargo. He told Duncan that the Colonel had contacted his agency after he had delivered his son to DeLouche college and that the agency had intercepted the signal that had been sent to Lindsey Norov giving him orders to eliminate the defector.

"We arranged to meet here away from any obvious connection with the developing oil situation. It was just a coincidence that you were coming here – a coincidence that Norov used to his advantage."

Duncan put this information together with what the newspapers had reported in recent months: the death-bed picture of a Russian journalist denouncing the president; the installation of listening posts and military hardware along the Polish border, diplomatic sabre-rattling between London and Moscow; the closure of the British Council offices on the grounds that the woolly pullovered employees were working for British Intelligence.

"If we're going back into a cold war situation we'd like to know what the opposition's real intentions are. Colonel Smirka was going to provide us with that information."

"Why him?"

"Disillusionment. He'd seen what the authorities were prepared to do in Chechnya and Georgia. The whiff of old style Stalinism, mixed with tooth and claw capitalism. To a military man like Smirka this all smacked of anarchy. The ideals of the Brotherhood seemed to be the only hope but even that let him down in the end. He'd read his history – expansionism justified as protection didn't cut it anymore. He came to us out of despair."

Normally Duncan would have taken issue with an American criticizing another country's expansionist policies but he felt that this was not the time. He was still getting used to the idea that Lindsey North, far from being a harmless, if rather sexually over-active, colleague was in fact a hired killer with a white Russian ancestry going back to the Napoleonic wars.

The door opposite to where they were sitting opened and Inspector Grippe was ushered into the room where Colonel Smirka lay.

Duncan did not like hospitals. They reminded him of his father's death. In his last years his father had sporadic episodes of amnesia. This condition was linked to a curious proclivity for locomotive travel, a form of transport he was very happy to abandon when he retired and did not have to commute to London anymore. Then in his eighties he rediscovered a boyish fascination with trains. Choosing a destination at random he boarded a train and, at journey's end, wondered into the provincial town in which he found himself. These excursions were usually terminated by a loss of consciousness and a head contusion when he fell against a kerb stone or a piece of street furniture. He had been taken to A and E departments in various parts of the country following these episodes and Duncan had travelled to be with him to sit out the long hours before he was patched up and sent home. During these vigils his father and he had chatted amiably about this and that – this was quite normal for them, they had always had an affectionate relationship without the need for wearing their hearts on their sleeves. The week before he died, Duncan had been called to Crewe General to retrieve his peripatetic parent. This time he was determined to persuade his father to accept the wraparound home care that Social Services were offering. After an unintentional detour into the maternity suite he had found his father on a trolley in the main A and E corridor. As usual his father had apologized for bringing him out of his way and Duncan had accepted graciously, overlooking the fact that 'out of his way' this time involved a two hundred mile round trip. His father had then launched into an uncharacteristically personal account of his life in which he emphasized his failings as a father and as a husband. Duncan had tried to counter these remarks but his father became strident and eventually Duncan fell silent. He gave his opinion on family members both close and distant, embarrassed Duncan by delivering a eulogy on his character and rounded off by revealing that he was probably going to be imprisoned for failing to pay his poll tax. The following week he had been rushed to his local hospital, this time omitting the pleasures of travel. A vein had burst in his frontal cortex. When Duncan arrived his father was already dead. It seemed fitting that his last journey had been to the largest intersection of train track in the country and that he had chosen

Crewe as the place where he would put his house in order, reflect on his life and prepare mentally for the end. What was uncanny was that he seemed to know what was going to happen to him.

Inspector Grippe emerged from Colonel Smirka's room and spoke to the two policemen who had arrived to guard the Colonel's room.

"Mr Andrew, I must ask you to return to your hotel and await my instructions. A police car has been arranged for you."

"What about Colonel Smirka? Will he be all right?"

"We hope so. He has only regained partial consciousness and the poison has done some neural damage but he is strong and the doctors are cautiously optimistic."

"What was it?"

"A combination of curare and ketamine concentrate – enough to bring a horse down. Fortunately Smirka is a good Russian – almost indestructible."

The unmistakable wheeze of helicopter blades and the   powerful roar of an engine stopped any further conversation. A door at the end of the corridor opened and noise like a physical presence enveloped them. Four men dressed in navy blue jump suits and wheeling a hospital trolley came towards them. Duncan could see the helicopter through the open door, its tail lights glowing orange in the dark. The door to Colonel Smirka's room was held open by one of the men. The others positioned the trolley beside the Colonel's bed. Monitor leads were detached from his body and a drip line was removed and reconnected to a mobile unit. The Colonel was lifted onto the trolley and strapped into place. One of the men nodded at Inspector Grippe and the four men regrouped around their assignment. There was something robotic

about their movements that Duncan thought was particularly
sinister. Duncan looked at Colonel Smirka as he came past. He
raised himself on one elbow, his pock marked face yellow and
rigid with the residual effects of the poison. The Colonel seemed
to recognize Duncan and he tried to turn his head towards him
but fell back and lost consciousness. Colonel Smirka was placed
inside the helicopter, its blades becoming rigid. Warm air from
the helicopter's exhaust was blown down the corridor as the engines powered up.   The helipad was briefly illuminated by the
Cyclops light of the helicopter as it searched the air and then
swung away towards the outskirts of the city.

Inspector Grippe wished the bewildered Duncan Andrew goodnight and then turned his attention to finding Lindsey Norov.
In a sense he did not need to find him. Smirka was secure and so
Norov was no longer a threat. His cover as a harmless tutor in a
provincial English town was now blown and he would not be able
to resume his life there. His only recourse would be to return to
Mother Russia in which case he would be out of the Inspector's
jurisdiction. On the other hand, professional pride was at stake
and he did not want this Berezinist to get away scot-free. After all,
even in the agency, attempted murder was taken quite seriously,
particularly when it involved interfering with agency activity. He
dismissed the possibility that he had returned to Lucia Bignole on
the grounds that the little flat adjacent to her father's hotel was
too obvious a hiding place. He hoped that he had not gone to the
train station – the dangers of chasing someone up and down a
moving object were too well rehearsed by Hollywood films for the
less than youthful Inspector to relish. Circumstance had obviated
the possibility of escape by car. Perhaps Lindsey did not feel that
he had to escape. There was a loose code of conduct between operatives that shied away from unnecessary bloodshed. Quite apart
from the difficulties of body disposal and having to deal with
the legitimate authorities, there was a kind of respect between

operatives, whatever their ideological colour. Lindsey Norov and he had been on opposing sides with Colonel Smirka as the political football between them. Lindsey had lost the game and the Inspector had won – this need not create any hard feelings, or any burning desire to take revenge – particularly from the victor. But perhaps Lindsey Norov might be useful to the agency. It was this possibility that set the Inspector on his trail.

CHAPTER 39

LINDSEY LEFT THE OPERA sure that he had accomplished his mission. He had seen his victim fall and knew that a mixture of curare and ketamine was lethal. The theatrical nature of his operation had been pleasing. Booking the seat that would allow him a clear line of fire and from where he could retreat unimpeded had appealed to his sense of control over the situation. The fact that the opposition would be present at the time of execution was also satisfying. He had been pleased by his choice of weapon. Explosives and even bullets left such a mess but a dart was clean and undetectable at least for long enough to secure his retreat. The question now was where to go. Operations heightened his sexual appetite and the thought of Lucia's naked body under his hands led him to direct his footsteps toward her flat. However, when he considered Digit's possible reactions to killing Smirka his pace slowed. Hurt pride might lead Digit to take revenge, on the other hand he might be more concerned with explaining how his assignment had been taken from under his nose. On balance, he thought that it was time to use the safe house and await developments.

The old warehouse development was a familiar place to Inspector Grippe. It was where he had been the day he met Daphne Bowler. He recalled that he had made several arrests amongst the low life denizens of the city that day. He also recalled that he had seen Lindsey Norov going into one of the completed flats that were steadily transforming the old warehouse. When he knocked on the door of the flat he had been surprised by Lindsey Norov's willingness to open the door and let him in.

"You're a hard man to find."

"All part of the training," said Lindsey.

"You know he's not dead."

"That will be remedied."

"I think not, we've airlifted him to the American Embassy. He's quite safe now."

"Well; win some, lose some. All in the game, eh?"

"The dart – a nice touch."

"Thanks."

Both men faced each other without moving.

"So. The Brotherhood. The agency would like to know more."

"Are you suggesting … two for the price of one. That really would be a feather in your cap."

"Just a thought."

"I couldn't do it. Too much at stake."

"Quite."

"Anyway, you're talking to a cradle to grave Berezinist here. My family go back to the beginning."

"Yes, I've read your file. Let me see. Recruited while at Cambridge. In a punt on the backs, I believe? Champagne, caviar and the heady idealism of youth. You were studying History and had come across your family link to the Berezinists in the form of Captain Norov, a cavalry officer who harried the French rearguard on the Berezina in 1812. His detachment was there when the French burnt the pontoons at Studzienka and the Brotherhood was born.

"I left Cambridge a red rather than with a blue. I thought of myself as a latter day Burgess."

"Several trips to Moscow made you into a trained field officer and you settled into your life as a college tutor with a reputation for being nothing more dangerous than a lady's man."

"My, you do know a lot about me."

Lindsey looked down at his suede loafers and considered what to do next. Digit had known where he would be and had presumably come to kill him. He had failed to eliminate Smirka and this meant that Moscow would recall him and an uncomfortable debriefing would follow. Despite this he had no desire to die and so he considered his options.

"Are you going to arrest me?"

"Hardly."

"Then what?"

"This."

Inspector Grippe's reactions were not what they had been as a young man. Before he had time to point the gun in his pocket at any mortal part of Lindsey's body his opponent was upon him. There was a brief struggle and the Inspector saw Lindsey throwing himself at a blocked up doorway. This apparently foolhardy

action proved to be his means of escape. The thin ply board gave
way and Lindsey disappeared into the darkness of the old building. Inspector Grippe peered into an unlit vastness and heard
Lindsey's retreating footsteps clattering down an iron stairway.
He followed only to discover that the stairway ended some six
feet above the floor below. He jumped and landed without injur-
ing himself. Dim light came through grimed windows and the
floor was littered with the remains of half eaten meals left by the
squatters he had arrested some days before. Above his head a steel
girder ran the length of the area. A scraping sound made him turn
his head and he flung himself onto a rain soaked mattress in time
to avoid a heavy industrial hook suspended on greased wheels that
sped towards him. The hook banged against the wall at the end of
its run. The Inspector glimpsed the retreating figure of Norov as
he clambered up the side of a stack of packing cases and reached
a narrow ledge. The inspector managed to fire two bullets before
Norov hurled himself across a gap and disappeared again.

Moving forward, the Inspector saw the outline of two figures hud-
dled against the packing cases. One of them held a lighter flame
under a large tablespoon while his companion, his legs tucked
under his buttocks, rocked back and forth. Inspector Grippe recognized one of them and they wished each other 'Buonasera' as
if they were passing in the street. Deciding he would not be able
to manage the jump, Inspector Grippe followed his prey at the
lower level. He moved down a narrow intersection of passages
and emerged into an area where furniture had been manufactured,
the machinery abandoned to the rats who scurried away at his
approach. The Inspector leaned against one of the machines, his
heavy breathing loud in the surrounding silence. He considered
giving up the chase – the pursuit being fuelled now by no more
than adrenaline and machismo and perhaps something equally
primitive – a hunting instinct lodged in the old brain that civi-
lization had not managed to elide. Doug Digit had spent his life
acting out of this instinctive behaviour, it had become second

nature to him, and even now, when the benefit of age had made him aware that what he did was not necessarily a good way to live, its pull was too powerful for him to resist. He moved towards the light thrown by a wall of factory windows, the frames weathered and rusting. Lindsey had been waiting for him and when he struck the Inspector with the full weight of his body both men fell through the windows the lead framing yielding to their weight and showering them with splinters of glass as they fell through the air. The ambiguity of their embrace as they fell made it hard to see whether they were trying to help or destroy each other. Falling through a further panel of glass in a skylight they came to rest in a jumble of material that had been used to stuff furniture. Lindsey was first to his feet. He sprinted to what appeared to be an opening onto the street but realized too late that he was running off a ledge forty feet above ground level. Inspector Grippe had travelled half the distance and was in time to see the surprised look on Lindsey Norov's face as he turned like a swimmer in mid air. The upturned soles of his suede loafers disappeared from view as he fell to his death. The Inspector walked to the ledge and looked down at the young man's corpse. Lindsey's legs had been driven into his body by the impact so that his femur had burst through his skin and were now visible through a mess of muscle and tissue.

CHAPTER 40

THE REUNION BETWEEN LOUISA Bowler and her mother, which took place on the loggia of the Palazzo Bignole, had been an equal mixture of admonition and relief. Utter Hoppe had stood a little apart from the DeLouche party as Louisa was received back into the fold. He seemed ill at ease as his friend was hugged and kissed and made a fuss of as if this display of affection meant little to him. He pulled his shirtsleeves further out from his jacket and cleaned his glasses on his cuffs and waited for this show of filial and parental reconciliation to end. Duncan was struck by Louisa's apologies which seemed to have none of the craven quality familiar to him of the child who begs forgiveness. Rather, she was a young woman who managed to say sorry for any anxiety she may have caused without throwing herself at their feet. Utter, too, noticed this display of independence and approved. Louisa took Utter by the arm and drew him into the circle of her surrogate family.

"This is Utter. He's an artist."

There was a brief pause and Utter waited for a torrent of recrimination to be directed at him. After all, it was he who had taken

Louisa away from them, it was he who had led her through that first long night together, had embroiled her in his thefts done in the name of art and had made fools of them all when their tandem had led them a merry dance through the streets. Instead Utter was treated to a display of Englishness that left him unsure what their feelings were towards him. Duncan stepped forward and said

"How do you do? I think I've seen some of your work. The banner? Interesting idea. Let me introduce you."

The DeLouche party said hello one by one and that seemed to be that. Duncan had made no reference to the events involving Louisa and Utter; perhaps because more dramatic events had overshadowed their actions and made them seem minor peccadillos in comparison and perhaps because their safe return from the very real dangers they had faced was enough to silence a post-mortem for the moment. Indeed, such a conversation would mean telling Louisa about the death of Lindsey North and the poisoning of Colonel Smirka and, despite her new found assurance, Duncan did not think she was quite ready for that yet."

"Well, we can think about going home now. Daphne, over to you."

"Thank you, Andrew. I have arranged our return journey. We leave this evening on the night train to Paris."

Pandora hooked her arm into Steve's and beamed with delight.

"Daphne, I don't know how you do it. That just sounds fantastic. A triumph for Two Wheels Good."

"Not before time. Anything to retrieve my tarnished reputation. I'm afraid I've not been at my best."

Daphne drew Louisa to her and for a moment the daughter seemed to become the mother and the mother resigned herself to her daughter's care.

"Couldn't do a thing while this sausage was on walkabout. Poleaxed me. Felt rudderless."

Duncan reassured Daphne that they all understood and that now there was one final treat to look forward to they should return to their rooms, pack and get ready to leave. Utter, realizing that this instruction did not apply to him remained behind with Cynthia who seemed reluctant to follow the others. She had been looking at Utter closely and now beckoned him to sit by her.

"You seem to have had a real impact on Louisa."

Utter shoved his glasses onto the bridge of his nose and made no reply.

"I'm not going to lecture you."

"I don't have to stay here."

"I know that, I just wanted to know you a little better. I'm very fond of Louisa. Will you come with us, back to England?"

Cynthia became aware that she would have to deploy all her housemotherly skills with Utter if she was to make any headway with him.

"Tell me about yourself. Where did you train? As an artist."

"Why do you people always have to know information like that."

"You people?"

"People."

"You seem very angry."

"Oh my God. A therapist. Don't give me your psychobabble shit."

"I'm interested in you."

'Why? Why should you be? I have nothing to do with you, I don't need your attention. Leave us alone, you old people just interfere all the time. Find something else to control."

"This sounds like a credo, but a sad one. I was young too, you know. "

"I suppose you think we have been having sex."

"No, I didn't think that."

"We don't have to be having sex all the time, not like your generation."

"Oh, so you are different?"

"Yes. We are free from all that. I make art."

"And this art has meaning."

"Yes. It means we understand the con and we're not fooled by it."

"I like that."

"Don't patronize me. You don't understand. The art is to stay free, to stand back and see things as they really are, not as we are told to see them. That is … unreliable. We only rely on ourselves, the rest is shit. Those galleries I hate them, they are prisons full of people condemned to see things the same way, cultural convicts. They stand in front of pictures like zombies and not just in galleries, everywhere …

At what point Utter realized that he was speaking to his mother is unclear, but Cynthia had known that this was her son the moment she had seen his eyes – they were Doug's eyes and were altogether beautiful to her.

"Your accent, I can't make it out. It sounds Dutch."

"It is Dutch. If you insist, I am from …"

"Utrecht."

"Yes."

"And you were brought up by Dr Hoppe and his wife."

"Yes."

"And never knew your real parents."

"No. Don't touch me."

"Utter."

"Don't touch me."

Darling D

It's rained all day and I've been thinking about you and imagining you having a beer in some picture postcard piazza. I miss you. Things have taken an interesting turn here. Simon has decided that I'm all right and has started to talk. Sarah doesn't seem very pleased at this development and I'm trying to stay neutral. I've had the whole story - Dad deserted by Mum and left with two kids (Simon and his little sister), Simon is expected to share the domestic duties including childcare and, on top of that, to carry his Dad's failed ambition to be a doctor. It's Mr Granger the Pharmacist in Summertown. He didn't get in to Med school so did Pharmacy instead. Simon is now expected to succeed where father did not. It's as clear as day, poor boy. He doesn't know what he wants to do but he certainly doesn't want to be a doctor. Just call me auntie Claire. Come home soon.

Love Claire xxx

CHAPTER 41

THE STAZIONE CENTRALE WAS unusually busy. Extra ticket booths had been placed along the central concourse to cope with the increased volume of passengers that had developed as the fuel crisis deepened across Europe. Uniformed officials were to be seen speaking urgently into walkie talkies adding to a general air of anxiety. Where it was quite normal to see people hurrying for their trains it was now possible to discern something else in their movement, something akin to panic as they strove to escape to their homes in the city suburbs. It was ten o'clock at night but most of those weaving between the Starbucks coffee stands were commuters, copies of Il Figaro jammed in their armpits, the shoulder straps of black laptop cases trailing at their sides. The relief of finally getting to the station was tempered by the thought that there might not be space in their suburban train. Some seemed to have already encountered this final insult and sat disconsolately on their brief- cases speaking into their mobiles, recounting the latest episode in the odyssey of their homecoming to patient partners who would cover the evening meal and put it back in the oven.

In contrast to the other platforms, the one reserved for the night train to Paris was empty. The powerful engine with its sleek nose cone seemed to confer a kind of dignity on those traveling north, separated from the herd by the romance and grandeur of their journey. The DeLouche party had gathered their bicycles at the entrance of the goods carriage and Daphne Bowler, now recovered and her ebullient self once again, distributed bright orange labels to the group. The Two Wheels Good logo was splashed across the labels making it clear to whom the bicycles belonged. Daphne was firmly convinced that the labels would ward off any potential thieves and so they obediently tied the little cardboard talismans to their handlebars. They reached their reserved compartments to find one of them occupied by a large woman who appeared to be taking up permanent residence. She had arranged a display of cleansing creams, eau de cologne and make up powders along one of the bunks and on another had set out a voluminous pair of pyjamas. When Steve and Duncan opened the compartment door, the woman looked up at them from one of the bottom bunks, the remains of a picnic meal strewn around her. Their attempts at explaining that the good signora must be in the wrong compartment were met by stony silence. Finally, Steve held his ticket up to the woman who had glanced at it briefly , snorted and picked up a chicken leg from the heap of food at her side. Playing for time, she inspected it carefully, opened her mouth theatrically and began to eat. The two Englishmen took stock. The balance of proof was on their side and they had a right to claim their places, after all where else were they going to spend the eight hour journey to Paris? Their opponent, on the other hand, had clearly taken the view that possession was nine parts of the law and was not for budging. Steve suggested that they rush her, bundle her out into the corridor and sweep her unguents and other belongings after her. Duncan was amused by this boyish thought but counselled against it pointing out that the sheer volume of their opponent would obviate any possibility of rushing or bundling. They looked up and down the corridor in the hope that a guard might appear to add weight to their case. None appeared. Male pride and the niceties of a negotiated settlement now came into play. They asked to see the woman's ticket and were surprised when she passed it to them between greasy fingers. She began to hum. Steve said that this was a bad sign indicating her indifference to their claim, an indifference that became more profound when Steve pointed out that she was indeed in the correct compartment but that the date was wildly at odds to their current temporal position in this turning world. The thought occurred to them that this formidable female was a serial offender, possibly turning up every week just to annoy foreigners. Duncan put forward the theory that she was a sort of bag lady of the ferreria, a well dressed hobo jumping trains across the continent. Finally, a guard arrived and a touching mise en theatre was played out. Steve and Duncan had not thought it unusual for another passenger to be obdurate even in the face of solid proof and had expected the lady to complain and even be angry at the tourists who were, from her point of view, given unfair preference to her. In fact, what they witnessed was a pantomime of movement that showed that this was not the first time it had happened. The guard proceeded with great gentleness. Speaking softly he moved about the compartment collecting her things and helping her to pack away. Putting a filial arm about her shoulders he apologized to Steve and Duncan and shepherded the woman down the corridor and out onto the platform. The two men watched her go and felt ashamed at their flippant treatment of the gentle soul whom they had not recognized as someone deserving of their patience.

Steve and Duncan were manoeuvering around each other in the confined space of the compartment that they now had to themselves.

"Let's take the top bunks before anyone else arrives," Steve said.

Climbing onto their bunks they selected what they needed for the night ahead from their cases. When the corridor began to fill with other travellers they stopped and sat still in a proprietorial manner. A man appeared in the doorway and glanced at his ticket. He looked at Duncan and Steve in turn and then withdrew. When the guard arrived they offered him their tickets and asked if the train was full.

"Si. Ma non qui."

"That's a stroke of luck. I'll only have to put up with you snoring."

Steve pulled a wad of leaflets from his bag and began to look through them.

"Teaching resources, Steve?"

"Nothing like the real thing. Info. on Etruscan pottery will come in very handy. Oh, and I got this for Pandora."

He handed Duncan a book of essays by Giorgio Bassani

"I noticed she was reading The Heron so I thought she might like it. It's in English."

"Thoughtful of you. Claire and I must have you both round to dinner when we get back."

Steve laid out his pyjamas and placed his washbag and a travelling towel on them. He rolled the pyjamas into a loose tube.

"I'll leave you to it. Back in a minute."

Duncan thought this a very English procedure, ensuring that they both enjoyed a moment of privacy while they shed their clothes and made ready for bed. He imagined himself at the DeLouche Christmas dinner making a joke about sleeping with Steve and revealing that his pyjamas were of the finest Italian weave. He opened a whitewash case that Claire had given him after her last trip to her parent company in the States. The case had a square of leather stitched to its surface with the word Emirates and some Arab lettering carried out in pale brown. Duncan rested the case on his lap enjoying its compact shape; it was the very antithesis of his sprawling domestic life, crammed as it was with an accumulation of objects and oddments that came with children and a long married life. He ran his hand over the surface of the case and thought that here was life as it should be – none of the paraphernalia of attachment. He recalled reading Henry Green's autobiography that was simply called Pack My Bag – a title that was redolent with ideas of movement and escape, of shedding a life and embracing the unknown. He remembered nothing about Green's life but the title of his book spoke to him in a way that was at once disturbing and reassuring. Of course, he would not want to pack his bag and leave Claire and the children – life without them would be unimaginable, meaningless, even – but what other ways were there to pack your bags? Scraps of writing came to him from he knew not where – 'it is better to have loved and lost', 'the road less traveled', something about returning home and knowing the place for the first time and a line from Keats that he did remember: "Then felt I like some watcher of the skies, when a new planet swims into his ken". Duncan fidgeted and pulled the sheet from his bunk around his shoulders and hoped that Steve would not return quite yet. Was this a midlife crisis moment? Would he bid farewell to his companions in Paris and take the train to Marseilles to board a steam packet bound for Tahiti with nothing more than a brush and palette in his bag; a modern day Gauguin leaving a trail of emotional wreckage behind him? No, that would not do, was not, in fact, what was needed. New planets, packing bags, journeys, transformations. He thought about the sketches he had written for the end of term college review and the way people had always laughed at the funny bits and complimented him on their success. He had never really taken these seriously but perhaps there was something there, some spark that could be brought on. And then his father came to him, or rather a mo-

ment after his father had made his last train journey and Duncan
had been clearing out his desk. He had picked up old cash books
where his father recorded the daily outgoings of the household.
The last pages of each book were covered in his spidery letters and,
at first, Duncan had assumed that these were notes about expen-
diture. On closer inspection he realized that the words were lines
of poetry. The cash books started before the war and ended in
the nineteen sixties. The poems brought together the momentous
events of those years with domestic detail and his reflections on
life in general. Many of them were overly sentimental but showed
Duncan a side of his father that he had never glimpsed during
his lifetime. Duncan assumed that his father thought there was
something shameful about this secret writing and so had only
committed his thoughts to paper in the privacy of his domestic
accountancy knowing that no-one else would be likely to read
them. His thoughts about his dead father were interrupted by the
return of Steve.

"Very attractive, you should wear head scarves more often." Steve
said returning from the washroom.

"What?"

Duncan realized that he was still gripping his sheet around his
chin. He shook it off his shoulders and jumped down from his
bunk. Steve jerked his head in the direction of the washroom.

"Don't go to the one at that end – someone's flooded it and the
lock's broken. They must have laid it on specially for the Brits to
make us feel at home."

Duncan pulled the washroom door to and a light above the mirror went on automatically. He turned the lock anticlockwise and
faced the mirror. The train began to move and he gripped the
side of the basin in anticipation of sudden, uneven movements.

When none arrived he loosened his grip and inspected his face. The harsh light revealed the extent to which Duncan had been deluded about his newly grown beard. He had thought that it would give him a grizzled and adventurous appearance – a man of the world who had seen a few things in his time. Instead what he saw was an aging face half hidden by facial hair that had grown unevenly and without any of the glamour he had hoped for. It was time it went.

Duncan unzipped the washcase flattening the two halves. An antiseptic smell rose from the case as he inspected its contents. The bag was divided into cloth pockets, each one holding an essential item for the executive traveller: Roger and Gallet Eau de Cologne (unopened); Colgate Plax to freshen the breath (also unopened, Duncan considering that toothpaste would keep his breath fresh enough); a roll-on deodorant (almost empty); Gillette shaving foam (unused); a safety razor still in its cellophane bag. The last pocket held a hairbrush and a toothbrush. Both of these items were short and hinged in the middle and gave Duncan particular pleasure each time he used them. He smoothed white foam over his face and unwrapped the razor. There was something about miniature objects that he found particularly satisfying: he couldn't decide whether it was the clever hinging or the Lilliputian size of them that was more pleasing. Simon and Sarah had both liked miniature things and he supposed that this was characteristic of childhood. He remembered how Sarah would sit for hours inventing scenes with her Polly Pocket, a kind of mimicking of the adult world, a rehearsal for the real thing. Sarah sometimes invited him to be an audience in these dramas. At these times he had been struck by her intense concentration as her imagination wove situations which had to be worked through and resolved and how they often involved a crisis that drew on each of the little figures invented personalities – their selfishness, or bad temper or greed – so that it was often like hearing a morality play unfold as the figures got their comeuppance and blame and reward were apportioned. Duncan finished shaving and thought about Sarah's play and how, when he wrote his sketches with Steve, it was like playing too. He packed the washcase, drew the zip slowly over the little items and held it gently to him as he walked back to the compartment.

Sometime in the night Pandora awoke from a dream in which her mother was chasing her down a road waving a bundle of papers and shouting at her. Pandora lay on her back and tried to remember what her mother had been saying. She stared at the dim nightlight above her bunk and was unable to recall any words, only the tone of recrimination remained and it was this that she now brought into her conscious mind. Turning on her side she wiped the misted window and looked out into the night. They were passing an oil refinery somewhere in northern Italy, orange flames vivid against the black sky. She had not thought about her mother since the day Steve and she had shared their food in the piazza at Montepuliano. It was this movement of her fingers on the glass that brought other times to mind. The previous summer she and her mother had gone to the family caravan at Lytham and spent a week there trying to enjoy themselves. Pandora had woken on the first morning and performed the little ritual that she always did when they were staying in the caravan. She turned onto her stomach and drew her fingers over the misted glass to see what the weather was doing. If it was sunny, the view through the pine trees to the sea would sparkle and the day would be full of possibilities, a drive to Poulton-le-Fylde or Fleetwood to eat candy floss and sit on the beach with a traveling rug tucked around their knees. If it was raining then they might go as far afield as Preston for the shops or to Blackpool to see if the weather was any better further north. It never was. So they would have a brisk stroll along the front followed by lunch at the Metropole.

Pandora tried to go back to sleep but couldn't. She lay listening to the steady swish of the train as it moved over the welded track, the sound of a clarion bell receding into the night. Switching on her reading light she picked up a worn copy of Wuthering Heights and read a few pages, became irritated with its tone of girlish hysteria and closed it. She looked out of the window at a quick succession of forestry and field and hamlet as the train sped through Torino and imperceptibly turned towards the tunnels of the Haute Alpes and Grenoble. Paris was now in front of them but still three hundred miles away. She thought about Steve and the boy who had kissed her all those years ago and mourned for a life lost and felt a kind of dread rising in her when she thought about the future and whether there would be one with Steve and if there was how she would cope. They had spent very little time alone, even when the events that swirled around the Palazzo Bignole had been happening there was always Daphne Bowler or Cynthia Digit somewhere nearby to dilute the situation. She had begun to notice things about him that she liked, his quiet manner and the concern he showed toward Daphne Bowler as she fretted about the absent Louisa and how he had been a voice of media-tion when the girl had finally turned up. She was not unaware of him physically either and found herself admiring his strong hands and the way his eyes had a habit of coming alive when he was speaking about the Greeks or some arcane piece of knowledge about Roman military campaigns. On the day of the opera she had come out of her room and seen Steve across the internal bal-cony, he was naked to the waist and she had recoiled at the sight of so much flesh. She knew that if things were to go any further she would be required to be with him physically and she searched her mind for anything that might help her and found nothing and was left with an unease and a certainty that she would disap-point him and that the companionship they had shared in recent days would be compromised.

The train slowed and come to a standstill. Pandora craned her neck and looked out. Sodium lights flickered on a man and a woman in the shadows of the empty waiting room. Unaware that they were being observed, the man undid the woman's blouse and, lifting her breasts free he kissed them in turn and moved his hands down her body. Pandora watched and imagined herself as the woman and Steve as the man who had now lifted the woman's skirt up onto her hips. He stood away from her and began to undo his trousers. Pandora's eyes were fixed on the woman who now lay back ready to receive her lover. When he came forward again all Pandora could see was the woman's stockinged legs waving on either side of the man's hunched body as he entered her. The train began to move again. Pandora blinked and wondered if her thoughts about Steve had conjured this image of carnal knowledge, a miasmic warning of the intimacy and invasion to come. She shifted her body down and pulled the sheet that covered her close about her face and closed her eyes and waited for sleep to take her away. And when it did she dreamed of waterfalls that showered pearls into a deep pool.

Cynthia sat alone in the dining-car and sipped her second Campari soda, a drink that was synonymous in her mind with holidays. She had awoken in the early hours and got up immediately knowing she would be unable to go back to sleep unless she moved about and did something. When this happened at home there was always a stray student returning from a night out to chat with but now, with her companions fast asleep, she went to the diner in the hope of finding a fellow insomniac with whom she might pass the time. Cynthia peered out of the window past her own reflected image and saw the outline of hills diminishing to rolling countryside; the last of the Vercors was now behind them giving way to the plains of the Isere. The sound of compressed air opening the interconnecting door between the carriages announced the arrival of another person. Cynthia looked at Doug Digit and said:

"You didn't tell us you were coming."

"Old habit. Information on a need to know basis only."

"So why are you here?"

"I wanted to see you safely home."

"Oh God, we're not still in any danger are we?"

"No. Actually I was coming to London anyway."

"And I don't suppose you can tell me why."

"No. Look, we need to talk."

"Do we? I can't decide whether we do or not."

"Ok. I'd like to talk, want to talk, put things right."

"That's very optimistic of you."

"Is it?"

"Quite apart from the shock of discovering you were alive and that you had been working for an organization responsible for some of the more morally outrageous developments in modern geopolitics, I have lived my life in your shadow and now I find it was all a lie."

"I don't feel good about it."

"When the patrol man arrived at our place and told me you were dead, I went numb. Nobody I knew had died. I didn't know how to react. But after a while I was angry that you'd left me, that I was alone, that you had been careless and got yourself run over, even. When I missed my period and took the pregnancy test I wanted to get rid of it but knew that the baby would be the only bit of you I'd… well, I was angry and I mourned for you through my anger."

"I always kept your picture. I asked to come back near San Verino because we had spent time there. It made me feel close to you."

"There was another way to be close to me."

"I couldn't do that."

"Higher priorities."

"At the time, yes, I suppose so."

"And later. After all there has been a lifetime."

"By the time I was settled here it was too late. I didn't imagine you would want anything to do with me."

"You knew where I was?"

"Yes."

"You could have come."

"I thought about it."

"You knew about Utter."

"I knew you had travelled to Bucharest. I remember worrying that you were flying so near your time. I had a contact in the city, someone I'd been in Vietnam with, he kept tabs on you, made sure you got into the best hospital. He gave me reports on how you were getting on."

"Reports. Did you file them somewhere?"

"Please," said Doug.

They had reached the outskirts of Lyon and the train clattered over a series of points and slowed, the suburbs shadowy in the early light. Shift workers could be seen in the empty streets returning home and a van waited at a level crossing as they passed.

"I had been to a lecture about dialectical materialism - pure propaganda - and I was walking back to the hotel when I went into labour. The ambulance that came to get me looked different to the battered versions I had seen on the streets – your friend laying things on for me, I suppose. The hospital was out of town – it was built to the usual soviet block design and smelt of camphor. The staff all looked like Olympic shot putters, all except the doctor who looked after me."

"Dr Hoppe. He was working under a government licence doing some research on malnutrition. He was only there for a year. It was lucky really."

"I was wheeled into the maternity ward. It was just a big room with some dirty looking cloth screens. I could hear everything, it was like being in a torture chamber. Women mumbling and screaming and nurses running about between us clattering bowls and instruments and one of them smoking a cigarette with blood on her apron. And then Utter came. I was told it was an easy delivery considering it was my first. He was only little. I heard Dr Hoppe say it was a boy and that he was four pounds and three ounces. Four pounds and three ounces. They wrapped him in a towel and took him away. Then they moved me: I was in a room on my own, there was a picture of Stalin on one wall and I could see the hospital garden out of my window. I asked to have my baby but they said that was not allowed, they expressed my milk and said he was being well fed. They kept me in for four days and Dr Hoppe came to see me every day. I tried to get him to bring the baby but he said that wouldn't be possible. We talked about me and what I was going to do. I didn't know how I could keep the baby, there was no-one to look after me, I didn't have a job. He said that I wouldn't be able to look after the baby properly and the best thing was to give him up to a good home. I was very young and he seemed so sure about what he was saying and when he suggested that he and his wife could give the baby a good life I just agreed."

Doug Digit took up the story. "It took them two months to get him released into their care, by that time they were leaving Bucharest and they took him home to Utrecht. He was christened Utter Douglas Hoppe. He went to school in the suburban neighbourhood where the Hoppes lived and grew up speaking Dutch and English. Dr Hoppe thought this was important. He worked as a consultant in the city hospital and Mrs Hoppe was a housewife. They had a house on the Friesland coast for holidays and weekends. Utter was always sketching, even as a little boy. When he was sixteen Utter had a sort of breakdown. He became very withdrawn and quite destructive.

"Who was sending reports this time?"

"No-one. I was in touch with the family. It was part of the conditions for their adoption."

Cynthia did not understand but wanted him to go on. She wanted to know more about the angry young man who had refused to acknowledge her at the Palazzo Bignole and who had rejected her proposal to come back to England with them.

"One day he went upstairs and threw everything in his room out of the window. The Hoppes didn't know what to do. When they were called to a downtown police station because Utter had been caught vandalizing parking meters with a pair of industrial metal cutters they decided that they needed help. A condition of his return home, rather than going to a reform home, was to see a therapist. The Hoppes were against the idea but I made them agree."

"Psychobabble."

"What?"

" When I spoke to Utter he accused me of using psychobabble on him. I'm guessing the therapy didn't work."

"He went to the therapist but made up dreams just to pass the time. Things did not improve. Later that year he ran away. The police were contacted but he was too old for anyone to be really interested. He just disappeared."

"I have a feeling you are going to tell me he didn't disappear altogether."

"It took me a long time to find him. He lived in a squat for a while. It was a bad place, most of the drugs that came into the city went through the squat first of all. I got him out just before a big bust."

"And how did you do that?"

"I took him off the street."

"In person?"

"Yes."

"Did he know who you were?"

"No."

"And now, recently?"

"He knows."

"He knew me too."

"He saw your picture in my flat."

"Yes."

Cynthia and Doug looked onto shadowy emptiness as the train drew north over the Rhone and on to the Maconais and knew that, for a second time, they had lost their child.

"The only thing he had with him was his sketch book. I was no judge but it looked pretty good to me. He'd made sketches of the people in the squat, they were like Goya's war pictures, horrific. I took him to an atelier in Amsterdam. They liked his work; they even seemed to like him, God knows why. Anyway, he stayed with them. He picked up work in the town, did some teaching with an art club. He lived independently."

"Did you go on seeing him?

"There was no need."

"No need."

"No need."

"Who did he think you were?"

"I told him I was in the police force and that he'd better do as he was told or he'd be in big trouble."

"And he didn't know then who you were."

"He might have done but he never said."

"And Italy? I suppose you know why he was there."

"No. That was just a coincidence."

The train ran between hillsides spiked with grapevines, the early light turning the land a luminous pink. Boards set up on the edges of the vine fields advertised the local wines. Cynthia finished her Campari and stood up.

"Thank you for telling me. Maybe he'll come round, when he's had time to think things over."

"Cynthia, do you want me to stay in touch?"

Cynthia looked into his eyes and could still see the young man
Doug had been and it was to this memory of his earlier self that
she agreed.

The train arrived in Paris Bercy and the Two Wheels Good party
transferred to the Gare Du Nord where they boarded the Eurostar
for London. In the minutes before they departed, a train pulled
into the platform opposite creating an illusion of movement.
When they did begin to move it was barely perceptible and was
accompanied by that feeling of relief and anticipation felt by travellers who put aside the tedium of the journey before them, and
experience an atavistic moment of release. For all of them it represented a distancing from lives they had, one way and another,
chosen to lead. Here was a moment when they glimpsed their
other selves free from the accretions of experience and inheritance.
Of course, they were not really conscious of this but they all felt
a kind of stirring. The trip to Italy was a watershed for them all.
In time, Utter found a way back to his parents; Pandora started
a new life with Steve in his Iffley Road flat; Cynthia returned to
Italy to throw open the shutters in Doug Digit's apartment and
forgive him and, once in a while, feed him Giafettis; Duncan
became a successful script writer, winning an award for his com-
edy series "Get Stuffed", a sit-com set in a taxidermist's office.
Daphne sold her travel company and started another one offering
her clients a week with any historical figure of their choosing; and
Louisa nurtured the little spark she felt every time she made a
drawing until it flamed out and allowed her to claim the world
for her own.